PRAISE FOR WOODY SKINNER'S
A Thousand Distant Radios

"Woody Skinner has a heat gun and he will strip the
varnish off your soul. You'll laugh while it's happening
and when he's done you'll feel more real."
—SCOTT SPARLING, author of *Wire to Wire*

"Reminiscent of other great voice-driven comic writers
of the American South: Barry Hannah, Donald
Barthelme, Padgett Powell … funny, sure, but also
capable of affecting pathos within the strangest of
premises." —BRIAN TRAPP, fiction editor, *Memorious*

Woody Skinner

A Thousand Distant Radios

Woody Skinner's work has won the Sherwood Anderson Fiction Award and appeared in *Mid-American Review, The Carolina Quarterly, Hobart, Booth, Another Chicago Magazine,* and elsewhere. He holds a BA in Southern Studies from the University of Mississippi, an MFA from Wichita State University, and a PhD from the University of Cincinnati. Originally from Batesville, Arkansas, he currently lives in Chicago.

WoodySkinner.com

A Thousand Distant Radios

stories

Woody Skinner

ATELIER26 BOOKS
Portland, Oregon

Cover design by Nathan Shields
Book design by M.A.C.

A Thousand Distant Radios
(Fiction)
isbn-13: 978-0-9893023-9-5
isbn-10: 0-9893023-9-3

Library of Congress Control Number: 2017942760

Atelier26 Books are printed in the U.S.A. on acid-free paper.

Atelier26

ATELIER26 BOOKS, an independent publisher in
Portland, Oregon, exists to demonstrate the
powers and possibilities of literature through
beautifully designed and expressive books that
get people listening, talking, and exchanging
ideas. We've quickly become recognized for the
excellence and idiosyncrasy of our titles, which
have been honored by the PEN/Hemingway Award, the
Balcones Fiction Prize, and the Flann O'Brien Award, and cited
on numerous Best of the Year lists.

Distributor: Small Press United/Independent Publishers Group
(IPG)

The valued support of Tina Alonso and Sidney Wade helped
make this book possible.

Atelier26 is grateful for grant support from the Oregon
Community Foundation.

Atelier26Books.com

For my family — in Arkansas and Chicago

Contents

A Thousand Distant Radios

Preferred Signals, 1985

G6: The East Coast News

We lived in a place where cable didn't exist. Our water was pumped from a well, our electricity streaming in on a TVA river wave. Dirt roads ribboned through our hills, where people were all but waiting on a filmmaker to document their poverty. We lived in Izard County, Arkansas, but we had a satellite dish in our front yard. A marvel of engineering, a jellyfish puffing toward the sky. Its frame stiff, shiny, a monument to mass communication. According to my father we were devotees of manufacturing, people who made an art out of industry. The satellite dish, the Buick, the trailer — our lives made of metals.

We were a space age family, my father liked to say.

He was an expert dish adjuster, a champion of signal. A skill born of practice, dedication, more than science. Out there in our front yard, in the space between fat oak trees, my father shaped masterpieces, our dish's antenna locked onto distant targets, sending pristine picture to our television. We watched until our eyes ached.

My mother died during the motherly act — that's how my father explained it. He was fifty years old when I was born. He cooked for the catfish buffet over in Strawberry. He liked to wear an old fireman's coat to the restaurant, chemistry goggles strapped around his head. He looked like a villain from one of the Mexican dramas piped in through the satellite. He looked like a fellow with an obscure but absolute capacity for destruction.

In the mornings, before I left for school, we'd angle the TV so we could see from the breakfast room. We usually watched the east coast news, reports from places fathomable only in two colorful dimensions, weather-map geography. My father liked to hear horror stories of the human variety, robberies and rapes and murders. He said we needed to hear them, that it was healthy to be reminded of our ugliness.

I would listen to the somber tone of broadcasters, their words drowned out by the sizzle and pop of fried meats. My father would pull baskets of meat and potatoes from the deep fryer, all of it soggy, grease dripping down your cuticles before dripping down your throat.

"What are we eating today?" I'd ask.

"Cheetah meat," he'd say.

One morning the two of us were sitting there staring at a New York weather map when my father said, "Looks like a heat wave's headed this way."

The map said the high in Buffalo was sixty-seven degrees.

My father walked into the kitchen, grabbed the pair of scissors he used for clipping fat from meat. He came back and faced away from me, staring at the TV. He raised the fat-caked scissors and cut into the shoulder of his plaid shirt, circling his bicep until he'd detached the sleeve. He unbuttoned the cuff and pulled the sleeve off, tossing it onto the kitchen table next to my plate. He was halfway through the other sleeve when he said, "Stand up, Edmund. You need some wardrobe adjustments."

I was fifteen years old, and I listened to everything he said. I stood before him and he appraised my clothes — a pair of khaki pants that were tight in the crotch, an oversized plaid shirt I'd taken from his closet.

He examined my shoulder, looking back and forth, right then left. He raised the scissors and snipped above my collarbone, gaining speed as he worked around my arm. He tugged the sleeve off and dropped it to the linoleum. I stood there quietly while he cut the other sleeve and trimmed my pants at the knees.

My father's eccentricity deepened during the last year of his life. Now, so many years later, I still have the satellite chart that hung over the mantle of our faux fireplace. Its markings are celestial, dots and pins angled into shapes, an astronomy of soap operas and sporting events, foreign films and public hearings. My father's scribbles crowd the edges, noting his favorite satellites, his preferred signals. It's easy to detect the absurdity, the nihilism, of his sickness now, looking back on his behaviors and obsessions. But in those days he could tell me anything and it was the truth. That, I've come to think, was my father's most damning illness: omniscience.

※

F2: Tennis

Tennis was always on, if not on a North American satellite then one from Sweden or Bulgaria. My father admired the sport for its uniforms, the tight shirts and short shorts and high socks. I tried to take up tennis. While other boys my age were mastering their skill with a chainsaw, fistfighting on the river bank, I was tiptoeing across weed-cracked courts, swatting the air with a racket, lofting the ball over the net to my coach. He was a man with a delicate beard and his loneliness surpassed his interest in my tennis skills. He'd stop halfway through a match to recite that week's supermarket specials, to describe the process of cleaning his gutters.

One afternoon I watched television from a folding chair while my father stood behind me with a hair clipper. Onscreen a couple of European men with scrawny arms and hairy legs were slapping a tennis ball back and forth, their shoes chirping on the court.

I could sense my father's distraction, the tennis match getting more attention than my hair. I sat there patiently, my father mowing a row of hair every once in a while.

"Be careful around my ears," I said.

"Shit, that ball wasn't anywhere close to the line."

He began cutting with a bit more vigor, the blade tugging my hair, releasing it.

"I have a scar from last time," I said.

"You're being dramatic," he said. "Cartilage hardly scars."

"Is this match point?" I asked. I'd been playing the sport for a year and still struggled with the subtleties of scoring. The European broadcasts could hardly help.

My father moved in front of me, lifted my chin to look at me.

"This may be my best work yet," he said. "I've highlighted your McEnroe qualities. Long enough to be rebellious but not so long as to affect your performance. Style *and* substance — that's the ticket, Edmund."

I heard the screen door swing open, heard someone padding toward us over the trampled carpet.

"Is it time to go already?" my father asked.

"It's ten till five," a female voice said. "I don't want to listen to Randy bitch."

It was Annette Meyer, a girl so pretty she made my breastbone ache, a quarter-sized pain that lasered through to the meat of my back. Annette had buck teeth, an almond-shaped dimple in her chin, black hair so thick it must've strained the muscles in her neck. She had a couple of years on me in school, and she had the rumors that kept me sleepless at night, squirming around in the heat of my sheets. She waited tables at the fish restaurant and sometimes walked to our place for a ride to work.

She stepped in front of me, stood next to my father. I kept my eyes down — she was too much to take in up close. These glimpses of her outside of school seemed thick with intimacy, with private knowledge — her high heels replaced by worn Asics. Her scent — Dial soap and bugspray — made my hormones roar.

She stared at me for a long moment, what felt like minutes, before she said, "It's a little bit lopsided."

"Yeah, it is," my father agreed.

"He has expressive eyebrows," she said. "Sort of like a young Louis de Funes."

She'd spoken about me before speaking to me. I'd never heard of Louis de Funes, but the name, coming from those lipstick-thick lips, somersaulted between my ears.

When the two of them left, I sat there looking at the television, listening to the whap of tennis rackets.

F4: The Sex Channels

The mailman was a woman who wasn't my mother. On the weekends my father would travel with her to Memphis. While he was gone, I'd spend most of my time in front of the television. One of the few frequencies I'd memorized was the F4 satellite — it delivered the sex channels to our living room. Watching them was like witnessing the events of a history that hadn't happened yet. Those onscreen bodies, slick with sweat and oil and other barely fathomable lubricants, popped together with gaudy pleasure. The women panted raspy falsettos, the men grunting from time to time.

I wouldn't call it arousal that I experienced watching the onscreen sex, not exactly. Not compared to what I felt in Annette's company. I was desensitized to the television, having spent so much of my life in front of it. My father said porn was a performance in which every moment was the culmination, the event we'd been waiting for. He said it was drama without the tedium of context, that it transcended the cause-effect paradigm. And nothing was more important to a boy's development than to abandon narrative morality, my father told me.

Late Sunday evenings, my father and the mailman would come home with bleary eyes and stiff bodies. My father, who talked about everything, who was incapable of discretion, never said much about Memphis. At the time I hardly gave it a thought, but over the years I've come to wonder if he was hiding something; if he was up to something he shouldn't have been or something that embarrassed him; if he was seeking some kind of medical treatment.

"What's Memphis like?" I would ask when he returned.

"Elvis and disco and pisspots," he'd say.

F1: French Cinema

Annette came over more often in those last months of my father's life. When my father stopped driving, she got her license, started making use of her mother's kelp Ambassador. The car was low and wide, a raft over the dirt roadway, and as she drove, gravel pinged into the undercarriage, her tires spraying the shoulders with grit.

Annette treated my father like a jarred firefly, like she better savor his every blink, absorb his last light. I did not share her awareness, her sensitivity. My antenna was focused on Annette. She'd all but moved in with us. At first she slept on the couch, a thin tee-shirt stretched over her beautiful knees. I coveted that curving cotton, pulled taut over her thin body. I hurt for her with vigor and virginity, blood humming through my limbs, jaws grinding in their sockets.

They spent evenings in front of the television, the satellite tuned to a station that played French films. They'd sit on the couch Indian style, their knees rubbing, mimicking the roles they saw onscreen, interpreting the lines. They'd laugh at the dramatic moments, the actors' expressive faces. Sometimes I'd march up to the recliner and plop down as though it was nothing to have Annette Meyer right there next to me.

But I could hardly breathe. I certainly couldn't talk. I'd stare at the screen. The French people communicating big feelings. The depth, the emotion of their faces, the fluttery octaves of their voices — I wasn't sure I would have understood even if I were a Frenchman.

It's still difficult to fathom Annette's presence in our living room. Sure, she yearned for our television, for the international programming, but it was always more than that. My father had a way of bringing the world, the things he wanted, close to him. Perhaps it is naïve of me, but I believe, even now, that nothing more than companionship passed between them. That they were simply magnificent friends, people who shared a sensibility, who bonded as they breaded fish filets.

❈

G1: Politics of the Soviet Union

One night we watched the live broadcast of a Soviet congressional debate. The Soviets argued with dramatic hand gestures, flecks of spittle bursting from their lips. "This is beautiful," my father kept repeating. "This is governance. These men know what it means to be powerful."

"It's so erotic," Annette said, and then she and my father looked at me, laughed together. My father's lungs hocked, he laughed so hard.

Annette acted strangely all night, sexualizing programming that was otherwise sterile. Weather reports and suitcase infomercials, even the off-air rainbow stripes. The clipped accents of the Soviets were steady, reassuring somehow, and I fell asleep, while my father and Annette mumbled to one another. I woke up with Annette on my lap, my nose pinched between her thumb and forefinger, my pants clumped at my ankles. She pulled her skirt up her haunches and settled on top of me. Then she pummeled me with her pelvis.

When I finished she leaned back, rested on her arms, and looked at me. Then she raised her leg and kicked me. Her heel cracked my nose, blood filling my nostrils. She dragged my pants up from my shoes and led me to the bathroom. Blood gummed over my lips, crusted onto my shirt. She wetted a rag with warm water and gently scrubbed my face. She stroked the rag along my chin, wiping away the matted blood. I was lightheaded with pleasure, with confusion, with pain.

"I love you," I said.

I've said those words so many times since, but that was, as far as I can remember, the first time.

"I'll slice you to pig meat if you tell anyone," she said, and then she left me with the blood-soaked rag.

At the time I assumed Annette shared my strong feelings, but in the days that followed she went back to ignoring me, snuggling up to my father on the couch, the two of them whispering jokes again. And after he died she stopped coming over altogether. Last I heard, she was a draftswoman for an architectural firm in Little Rock.

For a while I wondered if my father put her up to it. If the sex was their way of distracting me, consoling me before I even needed consolation. And there was the other possibility, too — that she was the one who needed distraction. That she was avoiding her own sadness about my father's waning health, his shriveling figure.

Over time I came to believe her reasons hardly mattered. I came to believe that my father and I communicated through Annette, our love for one another channeled through her. How separate he and I were, always. He had his own kind of gravity, a force that pulled me into orbit, closer and closer, before I stabilized into rotation, circling him at a distance, never close enough to collide.

G3: Dobro Jutro, Croatia

This is what I remember of my father's death: that it happened during the leftover broadcast of a Croatian morning show. The anchor was a blonde woman with a boy's haircut, a white dress gripping her body like cling wrap. The show had ended and she was seated on a beige couch eating noodles from an oversized bowl.

I called my father's name — he liked leftover footage, and he liked blonde women.

A crew member entered the frame, headset clasping his neck. He spoke to someone offscreen.

I called my father's name again.

The crew member approached the couch. Then he leaned over, kissed the woman on the cheek.

I waited for my father to return, as he always did, to the television.

G4: Dallas

I'd come home from school hoping to watch reruns of *Dallas*, and my father had taken me into the front yard, to the foot of our satellite dish. This was about six months before he died. We stared up at the sweeping rim of the dish. Up close it was big, sprouting between the trees like a giant flower, a steel lily. My father had never summoned me to the dish. He had always handled it on his own — always regarded attentions to the dish as a crucial part of his parenting philosophy.

"Why are we here?" I asked.

"Last night's storm," he said. "It knocked the dish off balance."

It looked fine to me, though I didn't know what to look for. My father placed his hand on the rim of the dish and held it there, as though he were taking its pulse.

"How do we straighten it out?" I asked.

He just stood there, staring past the dirt road into the broad field of sage across from our property. He seemed to be considering something vast and unknowable, how our television reception was affected by the steady expansion of the universe, maybe. I waited for him to say it. I waited for him to deliver one of his theories, one of those clever excuses he'd told me all my life.

"Should I crank this handle?" I asked.

"I'm dying," he said.

I nodded, but I didn't believe him. I'm not sure I ever believed that he was dying. It was always so difficult to distinguish between my father's truth and the actual truth. Only in time would I understand that, standing there in the matted weeds below the dish, my father had announced a truth unsullied, that he'd sent the message as clearly as he could.

"I am going to show you how to do this," he said. He aligned the dish with a distant barn, and then began cranking the handle. The dish tilted back, squeaking. "We're trying to connect to the G4 satellite. You know where the G4 satellite is — you've seen it on the chart."

I watched while his forearm circled, the antenna angling toward the afternoon sun.

✵

F4: The Pittsburgh Pirates

When I'd asked my father why he quit the restaurant, he told me the grease spoke to him, a language of sizzles and pops — that one day as he stood over the fryer the grease finally said, "Stop." It was important to listen to the messages the world delivered, he said.

He stopped cooking altogether, even at home. I was left with frozen lunches and store-bought sandwich meat, with white bread and mayonnaise. For a while my father craved salads. The mailman brought over heads of lettuce, stacked them in the fridge. My father would peel the leaves apart and eat them one ragged layer at a time, dipping them into saucers of ranch dressing. One day I opened the fridge and found a single rotting head, its leaves brown and shriveled as pond weeds.

"When's the mailman coming over?" I asked. "You need some lettuce."

"I'm done with the mailman," he said, "and I'm done with lettuce."

He had quit eating altogether. He looked like a dogwood during winter. He spent most of his time in front of the television then, but he'd stopped adjusting the satellite, stopped changing the channel. He settled for mainstream programming I knew he despised — cop shows and legal dramas and baseball. He'd point to the screen and say things like, "This is vulgar, watching these Americans butcher their own game. If I were a player I'd go play in Japan. Now *that's* baseball, their movements measured and precise. Chicago Cubs and Pittsburgh Pirates — this is like watching overgrown schoolboys flail around, their swings all muscle, their throws all shoulder. American players don't have the inner peace necessary to play pretty baseball."

Every once in a while I'd find him sucking on coffee beans pouched in his bottom lip, mouth swollen like a light-hitting center fielder.

G2: Figure Skating

We were watching figure skating. A girl with tiny arms and hammy thighs skated around the rink, rising from the ice in spinning flourishes. My father lay on the couch coming in and out of sleep. Annette sat at his feet, flipping through a design magazine, occasionally glancing up at the screen.

"I don't really like skating," she said. "How do you know the judges aren't cheating?"

My father raised his head. "Trick sports are the purest form of athletic pursuit," he said. "There are no rules confining the athletes. They are bound only by the limits of their bodies and their imaginations."

And then we lost signal. The screen turned blue, its bewildering light shading our walls. None of us acknowledged the loss out loud. It seemed an impossibility, the three of us in that living room without any signal.

I knew what needed to be done. I went outside. When I reached the receiver, I cranked the handle, adjusted the angle. I checked the living room window, hoping to see flashes of color, but the glass was tinted blue. I pushed the dish around, aimed its antenna across the sky, and still the blue remained. When I found nothing, when it seemed like I'd exhausted every starred corner of nighttime, I stopped.

I stood a moment looking at the dish, pressing my hand against its rim. Its surface was dotted with cool dew. I leaned against it, testing my weight, before I pulled myself up into the metal basket. I reclined there, my back cupped by the curved walls. Above me nighttime was a cluttered room, the moon chipped and swollen, stars dusty around it. I lay cradled in the dish, staring up into those greater, more resilient bodies. Then I stiffened myself and waited for signal.

Things in Slow Motion

We've never liked your house. Our houses have sharp angles and bright colors, cramped spaces and narrow stairways. Our houses sit on the edge of town, made of brick and vinyl siding, squares of yellow grass in front of them. We live in homes with trunked columns and wide windows, white mansions in the middle of green fields. We live in metal rectangles down by the river, trailers that slump on cinder blocks, pink insulation hanging from holes in their sides. But your house is modern — its profile low, its color muted, a gray that blends with overcast skies. Built sixty years ago by an architect our parents didn't like, your house sits on the edge of a bluff, an affront to the best view in town.

Right now you're enjoying that view from your freshly stained wooden deck. You recline in a musty nylon chair, smoking a cigarette and sipping diet cola from an insulated mug. We know what happens inside your house. Currently a nurse with permed gray hair and enormous bifocals waddles through your kitchen. Her name is Diane Simpson and she's one of us. Your older daughter is sleeping through her alarm. If you focus, if you listen very intently, you can hear it beeping. Your younger daughter has already left for school: she's turning left right now by that gas station that's also a Mexican restaurant.

We know all about you. More than we probably should. Don't bother looking for us, trying to confront us. You won't find us peering through a crack in your privacy fence; you won't find us staked out on the sun-hot shingles of your roof. We are the citizens of Batesville, Arkansas, and, excluding your family, our population is 9,447. Ours is a knowledge that transcends the limits of infrastructure and technology, that transcends the observations, the thoughts and feelings, of any one of us.

But this story isn't about us. It's about you. From the deck you're sitting on, morning looks like this: streaks of amber crowning the hilled horizon, coloring the gray of lingering night. You stub out your cigarette and immediately pull another from the pack. Two cigarettes before breakfast. You started smoking long before your wife got cancer but now you use her sickness as an excuse. Smoking is not your only habit that falls into that category — her cancer has given you an excuse to be yourself.

We are not interested in your wife's cancer. We stopped paying attention to her after the third relapse. We have our own cancer stories. We have families. Some of our mothers and fathers, our nieces and uncles, our brothers and cousins — they have cancer. We have plenty of cancer in our lives without peering in on yours.

Emma, the older of your two daughters, is finally awake. She slides open the glass door, lugs a chair across the deck to sit beside you. She holds her hand out, palm up, empty. Without a word, you tug the cigarettes from your pocket, slide one from the pack, and drop it into her waiting hand. You're not sure when she started smoking, but by the way she lights up, by the poise of the cigarette between her fingers, you're sure it's an old habit.

Emma is not beautiful, not like her younger sister, who resembles their mother. Emma looks more like you — bulging facial features and stringy brown hair, fair skin and fat ankles. It's something we talk about from time to time: how hard it must be for her to look so ordinary standing next to her sister.

"You're late for school." You say this flatly, like a comment on the weather forecast in a faraway city. It's her last semester of high school.

"Mr. Yarnell won't mark me tardy. He hasn't marked me tardy once all semester."

"How do you get away with that?" You ask this, even though you know.

"Cody signs me in on the roll sheet." Cody, the most recent in the series of boys who've marched through your house. Between both daughters, separated by a single year, it's hard to keep track of the boys. They all have sunburned skin and experimental wool on their faces. It's that age when every one of them takes on a redneck look, even the kids whose last names you recognize. It's that age when none seem fit for your daughters' attention. But still they get it. You stopped wondering a long time ago about your daughters' respective virginities. You can see in their posture, the way they lean on things, that there's no point wondering anymore.

You want to speak to her. You want very badly to confer some morning wisdom, something grandiose and fatherly, advice to make her day easier. Her week, her life. This is what you say: "I drove your car to the store last night. You need to have the tires rotated."

✿

We know how much you care about your daughters. Two weeks ago, you drove them to Little Rock for prom dresses, patient as they tried on one after another, as they agonized over colors and cuts. You've done everything in your power to make their lives normal, average, stereotypical. After your wife's relapse last year, you bought them matching black SUVs — sometimes we see them driving, their windows down, radios thumping top forty basslines.

We care about your daughters too. For years we've joined you in the softball bleachers, our faces dotted with sweat. Your daughters are terrible players. Their arms are weak and they drop pop flies and they swing at pitches in the dirt. We're surprised they haven't quit. But they like wearing the tight polyester uniforms and braiding their hair into thick pigtails; they like clinging to chain-link fences, chanting wildly while their teammates bat.

Your daughters are terrible players but, like you, we're glad they play. Anything to distract them from their mother. In those rare innings when they see action we scream their names, clapping as they step up to the plate. We stand beside you, slip our fingers into our mouths, and whistle so loudly your head throbs.

After Emma leaves for school you put on your scrubs and head to work. At the hospital you're not the husband of a woman with terminal cancer. You're not the father of two magnificent daughters. At the hospital you're a hero with a scalpel. Our hero. We come to you to have our gallstones removed, our hernias fixed. We come through the hospital's whirring electric doors, check ourselves in for the surgeries we've waited for.

We are the lifeless figures splayed in front of you, our limbs stretched across the cold operating table. Your scalpel splits the meat of our bodies, opens our insides: you see parts of us we've never seen, parts we can only imagine, and then, with delicate stitchwork, you seal us up. And afterwards, as we lay in recovery, listening to the drowsy patients moaning around us, you answer our vaguely ominous questions. You lean in close to the hospital bed, grab our hands, and tell us we're going to be all right.

This morning's surgeries are routine. Your hands work as though they belong to someone else, steadied by your intense detachment. After you're finished you move through the fluorescent sheen of the hospital's hallways, slowly regaining a sense of personhood, the fact that you're more than an instrument.

In the hospital cafeteria, greasy steam rises from hooded buffets. You grab a tinfoil-wrapped cheeseburger, a carton of fries, and push them to the cash register, where Mona Henderson smiles, waves you through.

You sit at your usual table, as far away from us as you can. It's in the corner, next to the gift shop that sells yellowing plants and slouching balloons. You bite into your hamburger, dip your fries in ketchup squeezed from dimpled packets. On the wall beside your table hangs a beige telephone, its stretched-out cord dangling to the ground. You pick it up, dial a number, wait.

The phone rings four times and a woman answers with a skeptical hello. "What's up?" you ask.

"Sitting at work. Looking over an application. This guy wants a two hundred thousand dollar loan for a racecar."

Normally you would listen, ask attentive questions. You like when she talks about her job because she likes when she talks about her job. But not now. You're too tired to be polite, to make clever remarks about over-draft fees and interest rates.

"Are you coming over tonight?" you ask.

She misunderstands, mistakes your fatigue for apathy. She doesn't say anything back.

"Are you?" This time your voice so layered with pleading that it's clear: you need her.

"Of course," she says. "What time do the girls leave?"

The girls. That's how she refers to your daughters. In your mouth the same phrase sounds affectionate, like you're in denial about the fact that they're growing up. In hers it sounds derogatory, like a reference to a pair of objects that stand in her way.

"They're playing out in Paragould. That means their

bus leaves early and gets back late. They'll be gone by four o'clock."

※

We don't know this woman (we'll call her your girl-friend) very well. Mary Beth Henry, the bank cashier who wears denim dresses to work every day, says your girlfriend grew up in Izard County, a place north of here where people scrape their lives out of rocky Ozark soil. She graduated high school in a class of fourteen; three of her classmates hadn't made it — meth, car wreck, murder. She's from that kind of place, a place very different from the quiet hamlet we call home. But now she's got a job at the bank and she's got you. A doctor. And not just any doctor — a surgeon from a good family, a surgeon with a view from Eagle Mountain.

For a while your infidelity escaped us. We have to admit you were pretty slick, staging the affair right under our noses. You'd walk past our houses at dusk, our windows flickering with television light, our dogs howling at your footfalls. After your wife of nineteen years got sick we didn't question your odd pedestrian tendencies; we didn't wonder why you'd suddenly taken to exercise; why sometimes you left on foot and stayed away until sunrise. Even when Leroy Jenkins, the former postal worker with the giant flagpole in his front yard, saw you walking down the street in the middle of an unrelenting downpour, your clothes sticking soggily to your body, your hair pasted into streaks that barely covered your glistening scalp, he was none the wiser. We — especially those of us less familiar with loss, who can't even begin to imagine what you've gone through — forgave your new habits.

But of course your affair could not go undiscovered, not in this town. You might have deceived the neighbors, and the Indian couple who run the Scenic View motel. But Melissa Risher, the waitress at that greasy restaurant next door to the motel — she recognized you. Years ago you did surgery on Melissa's ingrown toenail, a procedure you've long since forgotten. And one morning as she was parking she saw you emerge from a motel room with a woman who occasionally attends her Sunday school. The news spread quickly, whispered through pursed lips, passed cell phone to cell phone. It traveled between computer screens, midnight emails casting our faces in ghostly silver.

We can't say we were shocked. Not exactly. After all, we've heard about your occasional indiscretions, all the stupid things you've done in the name of love. Coach Wallace still talks about that time you skipped the game against Newport to meet Carol Carlisle behind the high school gymnasium. And we heard about that night in the Little Rock dive bar when a mouthy drunk disturbed your wife and you busted his head with a beer bottle, threatened to shred his fucking vocal cords with the bottle shards if he said another goddamn word. For you, love is a devastating force, an impetus to flamboyancy and humiliation, and to be frank, we've always enjoyed watching it wreck you.

✲

You usually walk the half-mile to the Scenic View, but today you're parked in the motel lot, waiting. As convenient as these meetings are, their novelty has dissolved. Sometimes she checks into a room, sometimes she drives you to her house. It's an apartment, actually. It depresses you — a small place in a newly-constructed part of town. With its dull brick and brittle siding, its electric security gate, her apartment reeks of self-satisfied compromise — it's the sort of place that impresses someone who comes from a background like hers, someone for whom life's basic necessities seem like luxuries.

But these motel trysts no longer gratify — you have spaces, more intimate parts of yourself, that you want to share with her. You want her to meet your daughters, to come face to face with the people you've made. A strange part of you wants her to meet your wife. Or the old version of your wife. You've idealized that version — you think she was so beautiful, charming, generous, that your new girlfriend wouldn't have threatened her. She might've laughed your new girlfriend off — some sort of mid-life crisis, an inelegant phase, like those conversations you had with the Bosley representatives about your thinning hair.

Just after five o'clock your girlfriend parks next to you. When she approaches your car you tell her to get in.

✳

You park on the street, a habit now, to make room for
your daughters' SUVs. You walk around to the
passenger side, where you clasp her cold hand. You
squeeze it, feeling the warmth, the pulsing heat.

In front of you crouches your house, a silhouette
embalmed in gray twilight. The sky sprawling behind
the house is blank as a movie screen after the credits
roll. Together you walk through the yard, grass still
glistening from a mid-morning rain. You stop before
you reach the door. You lean into your girlfriend and
she rests her head on your chest, her bony shoulder
digging into your ribs. You want to say something to
her, something quiet and meaningful, but instead you
point to the wreath hanging on the door and say, "My
daughters made it for Halloween." She doesn't mention
the fact that it's March.

When you open the door you're struck by the oddly
soupy smell of your home and family. And as you move
together through the shoe-cluttered foyer, through the
den with its mess of rumpled blankets and stained
pillows and empties of Diet Coke, you feel a wincing
guilt over the condition of the place.

But not even for a moment do you consider hiding
her from the on-duty nurse. In fact, you give her a tour,
tugging her through the kitchen, dining room, library.
You want to show her everything, every last room,
every last crevice. You lead her out to the deck, where
you stand staring together over the bluff.

After a long silence your girlfriend says, "It's like things are in slow motion down there."

She's right. From this vista there's an ethereal stillness, a tranquility about the world. It used to unnerve you, this vista, but you got used to it.

Heading inside, you lead her down a hallway lined with photographs you stopped noticing a long time ago. She slows, leans toward one: your family stands at the foot of a Colorado mountain. It's from a life you can barely remember, before the diagnosis — it's the time you wonder about the most, miss the most. Not because you were the perfect husband or father. You weren't. Need we remind you of the night you left the middle-school fundraiser with a bottle of cheap champagne and the first-year math teacher? Or the almost daily spats in front of the children, the time you ripped her grand-mother's clock from the kitchen wall and slammed it to the tile floor? No, you miss the way you felt before the diagnosis because you operated then under the illusion that you were in charge of your own destruction, not subject to some force crueler and larger than yourself.

"She really was as beautiful as I've heard," says your girlfriend, still looking at the photo. "Even after two kids."

You pull her to the end of the hall, to a pair of side-by-side doorways. One room is bright pink, the other bright green. Laundry blankets their floors, discards of last-minute outfit changes, a constant wardrobe war. In Emma's room a cluttered pinup board holds group photographs and magic marker notes and softball hair ribbons — the glossy artifacts of adolescence. In Sara's room the bedside table is stacked with books; she is brilliant in an unfussy way, like you in high school.

The last thing you show your girlfriend is the guestroom across the hall, the cleanest room in the house. From the foot of the guest bed you draw her onto the stiff comforter, your head on the hard pillows. Then you pull each other's clothes off, arms tangling and untangling, hands moving in practiced rhythm. The familiarity of this routine pleases you in a way it wouldn't have ten years ago — you were too naïve to ever feel this way with your wife.

※

She wakes you from an iron sleep and you are cold and heavy-blooded. The clock on the bedside table says midnight. You have no idea if that's right. You rise from the bed and peer out the window. The driveway is still empty. Your daughters will be home soon.

She begins getting dressed. "I wanted to let you take a nap," she says. "Guess I fell asleep, too."

You are standing together in your yard when you see the headlights. You stop, waiting for them to turn, pull into another driveway, but they keep coming. You look back to say, "hide," but she's already moving away, headed toward your neighbor's yard, toward the motel.

"I'll call you," you whisper, but she keeps moving through the darkness, making the same walk you've made a hundred times.

※

You're in the kitchen when you hear your daughters come in. They go directly to your bedroom to check on their mother, to tell her body goodnight. Five years ago, at the start of this nightmare, you tried to limit their worry. You thought it unnatural — little girls caring for their mother, meanwhile mimicking her cheery attitude. But now they're almost grown up. They're nearly women and there's nothing you can do.

In your kitchen you're reflected in every surface — the appliances, the countertops — all commercial-grade stainless steel. It was your wife's idea, this kitchen. She was a bad cook, the worst, and she knew it. She thought a restaurant-quality kitchen might help. It didn't.

You decide to cook some eggs. There's a carton in the fridge. Over a tall blue flame you set the biggest skillet you can find. The hot iron sings. Then you crack shells on the counter edge, split them over the pan, and stir with a burnt wooden spoon. The heat glares up into your face, the oil flecks your forearms.

A hand presses into your back and you turn. It's Sara, still in her softball uniform, hair pulled back beneath a headband. The uniform is spotless, pants a chemical shade of white, jersey crisp — she didn't get to play.

"Did you win?" you ask.

"Lost both games. Emma played third base in the second game, though."

"That's great," you say. "Any balls come her way?"

"No. Steph Maxwell was pitching so all the hits went to the outfield."

Emma comes in carrying her dusty cleats. She stands tall — a hint of her newfound importance as a second-game starter.

You tell her you're sorry, you wish you could've seen her in action, but she shrugs it off, says she didn't make any plays.

They sit side by side at the island while you cook, their cell phones in their hands, fingers flicking like instruments. You wonder if they know about your girlfriend. Maybe they sense something, maybe they've heard. Locker-side whispers or rumors from the teachers' lounge.

Trust us when we say this: they don't know. Not one of us, not even Stacy Westmoreland — the smug little beauty queen who plays second base — has uttered a word. The story of your girlfriend might as well be some esoteric definition buried in their science book glossaries. So primal, so animalistic, so human — your girlfriend story occupies a part of life completely unfamiliar to them, the kind of manmade tragedy they don't even know exists.

We don't have to tell you this is temporary. It might be a week from now, might be a month. You and your girlfriend are sitting outside on your deck, watery fast-food salads on the table in front of you. Above you, next to you, the sky a pastel blue, and she's telling you a story about a man who came to the bank and tried to withdraw his life savings — forty-seven thousand dollars — in quarters. Maybe she's near the end of the story, the part where for weeks everyone at the bank walks around coming up with reasons the man wanted the quarters: a lifetime of laundry to do, or a very large car to wash, or he really liked bubble gum. And then the glass door slides open to reveal Emma, or Sara maybe — one of your daughters steps out into the sunlight, staring, confused, until she realizes what she sees.

That moment is not your story's climax. Sure, it's what we will talk about. Whispers over cubicle walls, hushed voices in line at the supermarket, bourbon-tongued slurs at the country club bar: a moment subject to countless retellings, its characters and events and settings evolving to fit the audience, to satisfy our crudest desires.

But now is the moment we've reserved, the quiet culmination we want you to appreciate: you standing there with a spatula, sliding eggs onto your daughters' plates. They set their phones down, take up forks, and eat the meal you've cooked. You stand on the opposite side of the counter, eating the leftovers from the warm frying pan. No one speaks. Normally you would say something to overcompensate for their mother's absence. But now, for a singular instant, you remain silent, savoring the scrapes of their forks, the smack of their lips.

✻

When they've gone to bed you stand on your deck, leaning against the railing and staring over the bluff. Soon your daughters will be women and they'll want things from you that you cannot give them. And like their mother, like your girlfriend, like many of us, they will be disappointed.

But tonight. Tonight moonlight thins the darkness, gives the sky a dull transparency. Beneath you, lights fleck the rolling landscape with orange, like the embers of a dying campfire. You see the neon signs of restaurants and you see the monolithic bulk of the hospital and you see cars swimming along the highway like minnows into a stiff current. This is what you see: us. We're eating late dinners at fast food places and we're making our rounds in the intensive care unit and we're driving home from Wal-Mart. And as you stare down at us, our presence gives you a lonesome kind of comfort.

The Knife Salesman

Today is not about sales. Here at Cutcorp, we're interested in establishing long-term relationships. We're interested in community. So every now and then, we host a "Cutters of the Future" day at a local elementary school. This is one of those days.

I do my usual demonstration for the kids, the one with the rubber snakes and the tomatoes and the crash test dummy. I'm under strict contractual obligation not to sell to anyone under eighteen (part of Cutcorp's Safety-First Policy), but what happens between the kids and their parents is beyond my control.

When I walk out of the school gymnasium, there's a line of minivans waiting for me in the parking lot. Most parents already have the checks made out. To each and every one of them I recount the responsibilities of Cutcorp knife ownership. I tell them a Cutcorp knife will slice through a pinky finger like a soggy carrot. Still, when I hand over the knives, the parents toss them haphazardly into the back seat, into their screaming children's arms.

It's not uncommon for me to enchant parents with my passion for their kids' wellbeing. Today, five people — three mothers, two fathers — actually ask me on dates. Meanwhile their children stare at the blades, transfixed by their own icy reflections. I would worry, had I not spent the last half hour of the knife assembly talking about safety.

I'm a leading knife education advocate for our country's youth. I always say to parents: you can make sure your children brush their teeth twice a day, you can make sure they eat their green beans, you can make sure they're dressed warm in winter, but whatever you do, don't hide the knives from them. Because one way or another, in the world we live in, those precious, silky little hands will find their way to a blade.

❋

I serve a variety of cutting needs — from the local butcher's gory, blood-spattering hacks to the delicate dices of pearl-necklaced housewives. I've worked for Cutcorp seven years now, won the company's National Salesman of the Year three times in a row. It hasn't even been close. I sell what I want to who I want. I've sold butcher knives to blind nursing home patients. Field-dressing knives to card-wielding PETA members. Steak knives to San Francisco vegans.

It hasn't always been this way. I didn't always possess such talent with knives and people. I started in the Whet Your Feet program as a sharpener and, upon graduating, began my apprenticeship under a Cutcorp legend, one Doc "Wallet-Shredder" Henderson. Doc became famous in the knife sales world for his five o'clock shadow trick — he'd scrape Cutcorp blades down his bristled cheeks, shave himself in clients' living rooms, the black wool of his face wafting onto white, vacuum-crisp carpets.

On those long, hot, slow afternoons during my apprenticeship, Doc told me the legend of Jack McGregor, the patron saint of Cutcorp. McGregor had been a prominent New York City surgeon until one day, in the middle of an emergency appendix removal, infuriated by the dullness of his scalpel, he walked out of the surgery, walked out of the medical profession, walked out on his wife and two daughters, in search of a higher order, in search of sharpness. He sought steel that could glide through skin and muscle and bone. But when he found it, he wasn't satisfied. He wanted steel that could cut through everything. He wanted steel that could carve away the hulking mystery of the Earth.

❋

Today I have a house call with a woman I met while staked out at Starbucks. Her name is Hillary, and she lives in a tall, narrow Victorian in St. Louis's Shaw neighborhood, where rich people who like old things dwell. I feel like I'm on the set of a digitally remastered black and white movie. The houses are old. The cars are old. The people are old. Even the dogs they're walking look old, like they're just waiting around for the vet's needle.

When I ring the doorbell, a cleaning woman answers, invites me in. The ceiling is so high I have to squint to see it. The place smells like a drawer from the card catalog at my middle school. She directs me to the living room, where these cloud-haired old women await on overstuffed furniture. Their bodies are draped in earth tone clothing, beaded necklaces dangling over their blouses.

They discuss a book. It's a physical object, pages glued together at the spine. I am patient. I lean against the wall and listen to them talk about a pretend family named the Berglunds. I am bored until they begin to argue about whether the writer is a snob. A woman in a hemp pantsuit gets very emotional — she claims to have gone to elementary school with the author's aunt (he grew up in St. Louis, apparently). It doesn't take long for things to get ugly. The hemp woman bats another old woman's glasses off of her nose — that's my cue.

When you interrupt a geriatric catfight with boning knives in both hands, you get the room's full attention. I wheel my suitcase between the couches, lift it onto a coffee table shaped like the hull of a Mississippi riverboat. When I unzip it, the women sit down in unison, like a church congregation spellbound by the silvery gospel of its contents, the holy shimmer of the blades.

I stopped off on my way here and purchased a few supplies for this particular demonstration. I may drive an SUV and I may enjoy watching professional football on humongous high-definition televisions and I may own three different pairs of Oakley sunglasses, but I haven't made it this far without an uncanny under-standing of my market. I reach into my suitcase and pull out a burlap bag full of organic produce and Spanish wines.

Without asking permission, I line up a row of fruits, veggies, and cheeses on the big coffee table. I set the wine bottles on the right, next to a lush tomato. With my left hand, I chop my way down the line of food, halving the oranges and grapefruits and bananas, until the blade melts through a block of goat cheese. The rhythmic cutting, the sparkling tick of the knife, leaves the women entranced. They forget who or what that book is about. By the time I make it to the eggplant, they forget who or what *they* are about. I keep my left hand moving, punching down through the last of the veggies, while I raise a cleaver with my right hand and swing at the wine bottles. The blade sings through the glass necks and the decapitated tops drop to the floor. The bottles remain standing, blood-red wine spilling down their sides.

I look around the room. I have taken these women to a place more mesmerizing, more real, than anywhere their books have ever taken them. Their faces droop with the weight of what they have witnessed. Saliva drips from unhinged jaws. I sense their hunger, their longing, for the banquet spread before them. So I take a steak knife and stir all of it up — fruits and vegetables, wine and cheese. When I've got one big preservative-free pile, I stab the knife into the stack, the food sliding onto the blade like a shish kabob. And without saying anything, as if instinctively, the old women crowd around me, their mouths open, ready to eat from the blade. I know — they know — that with even one small miscue, a tongue will sever and drop to the floor with a slobbery splat.

✳

My first two big breaks occurred on a single night five years ago. I was at P.F. Chang's on my first date with Mandy. The service was good, the lighting was low, and the music was unfamiliar but cool. The only problem was the cutlery. It was mid-grade at best. A few months earlier when I'd talked to Jimmy the manager about upgrading to Cutcorp, he'd laughed me off and said silverware operations were handled by the corporate office in Scottsdale, Arizona.

My date was going well. Mandy and I were telling each other work stories when I noticed her struggling to cut a piece of chicken. Something inside me, something primitive and protective, snapped. I unsheathed the BuckBuster Pro I wore on my belt, lunged across the table and, with a quick flip of my wrist, sliced the chicken into strips. Mandy was dumbstruck, but her face reddened with gratitude.

The people around us stopped eating. One by one, they set down their silverware — an impulsive protest of the blunt mediocrity of their utensils. I've never wasted an audience, so I stood on my chair, raised my Cutcorp blade above my head, and demanded a boycott until P.F. Chang's rectified the unforgiveable dullness. People began to stand up as I talked about tired wrists and inflamed arthritis, struggles with tough meat and knotted noodles. They stood slowly at first, but soon they were rising into a standing ovation. In the middle of the crowd a man threw down his silverware, utensils yelping across the tiles. Soon pieces were clattering to the floor all around and the air thickened with silver as metal lofted overhead, glinting in the muted restaurant light. It could have been dangerous — for the first time, I was glad the silverware was dull.

Ten minutes later, Jimmy the manager, with permission from corporate headquarters, signed a contract guaranteeing P.F. Chang's nationwide implementation of Cutcorp products. I retrieved the emergency silverware I kept in my SUV and handed it out to customers. People returned to their tables, resumed their meals. And so, like the participants in so many great negotiations before us — those fateful pacts in faraway places like Plymouth and Paris and Versailles — Jimmy the manager and I had come together to end the St. Charles P.F. Chang's Rebellion of 2008.

Mandy and I married the next day, a small ceremony at the courthouse, our immediate families the only guests and the courtroom stars and stripes our only decoration. We honeymooned for three days in Joplin, where I stopped into a deer hunters' expo and sold an apocalyptic number of knives.

Nine months later, Mandy gave birth in the middle of the night. A boy, Jefferson Mills. Jeff, we called him. Sitting on the hospital bed next to Mandy, I held him for the first time. In my arms, his body felt harder, less fragile, than I expected. It radiated with the warmth that began in his mother, began in me. His breaths puffed like tiny whispers, tiny words that spoke the name of the world.

❈

Hillary, the host of the book club meeting, works for a local talent agency. She's decided I'm an act worth representing, so she's arranged something bigger than the house call. I keep telling her I'm a salesman, not an entertainer, but she insists I am both. She's rented out the Scottrade Center, where the St. Louis Blues play, and for the last two weeks, she's had cable ads running four times an hour throughout the entire metro area. She's named the event Cut-a-Palooza, and the ads have promised "live uncensored cutting."

The show starts at 2:30 p.m., but the parking lot is full by noon. Drivers are honking and screaming, their heads hanging out the windows. Thousands tailgate outside the arena. Classic rock blares, the afternoon air flush with the aroma of scorched hamburgers, the sweet vapors of domestic beer.

Just before the show begins I walk down a long tunnel toward the arena floor, rolling my suitcase along beside me. I stop to wait on top of the red X, like Hillary told me. From the tunnel I can see out onto the empty floor. The lights have been dimmed for a laser show; the arena blinks with my favorite colors — our favorite colors. Freddie Mercury's voice squeals through the PA speakers as the audience stomps and claps. My cue is the fog machine. Yesterday, in our final pre-show meeting, Hillary said that if I start a casual gait when the fog machine begins, the timing will be perfect: the bald eagle will soar from the rafters, out over the crowd, just as I emerge from the tunnel.

The fog machine begins its hiss, a bitter haze filling the tunnel, the floor vibrating beneath my feet, throbbing with screams and applause.

❊

Hillary and I sit in her cinema room, reviewing the footage, critiquing my performance. I began with my standard fruit and veggie routine, working in some knife juggling just to give them a taste of what was to come. Though it was a swooping blur of feathers and beards and clucks, I'd nailed the flying turkey decapitations, clipping all ten birds from the air in less than two minutes, their headless bodies gliding above the floor, blood streaking behind, fanning flecks of red onto faces in the crowd.

The film, projected through the crisp, dustless air of Hillary's screening room, plays with pristine resolution, my performance painfully vivid. I sit up in my chair as I await the final sequence. Yesterday, I wasn't sure the crowd was ready for the grand finale, the bullfight and subsequent butchering. And after I used the tee-shirt cannon to shoot a dagger through the bull's side, after the humane swipe of the beast's throat, as I cut the hide from the meat, I began to worry the scene was too gruesome. A dense pink steam arose from the blood-drenched organs, innards splayed across the cold concrete. But as I watch the film today, I see what the crowd saw, feel what the crowd felt. It is sad and strange and beautiful, I decide, all the things a good knife show should be. I made the audience feel things they had forgotten how to feel.

I say so to Hillary. She tells me yes, they must have felt something powerful — by intermission, the concession stands had sold out of knives.

❊

I'm two weeks into my nationwide tour, lying in a hotel bed in Albuquerque. I grip a knife in each hand, hold on tight while I toss and turn. The blades shred my cool satin sheets into gauzy scraps, tear up tufts of mattress, rip through feather pillows, until I've pieced together a nighttime nest.

I finally nestle into sleep and dream back to an old time long before me, a time remembered from childhood textbooks. I see St. Louis. I see Lewis and Clark. I see wagon trains heading westward. I see trappers and traders, pioneers of the real America. I see broad expanses of prairie, mountains that scratch the surface of the sky and, farther still, I see an ocean, the Pacific, just waiting to fill American eyes, to fill American bodies, with the electricity of its blue. I see space: vast and empty and wild. I see savages scattered across the land in small villages, overwhelmed and lost, waiting for Us to save them, to show them what God made this land for, what He made this Country for.

And St. Louis: oh St. Louis! That is where it all started, where people hitched up their wagons, watched their fears blow away like dust from a barren road, and set out to follow the blood trail of their dreams.

And sometimes, in mid-sleep, I smell it. The salty

musk of horses, the mildewed mud of river docks, the sour vapors of mash, the dizzying must of whorehouses. I smell prosperity.

And then I see the knives. Then I see me. I stand on a busy street corner with a wooden cart, selling knives long and short, Bowies and daggers, blades so fresh they're flame-warm, just carried over by the blacksmith. And a line of people stretches down the street, waiting. They hold things they're planning to barter, flintlocks and skins and sacks of flour. Some are more desperate. Some say goodbye to their children, prepared to trade the servitude of their offspring. I'm so swamped, I feel relieved to have the help.

It's wonderful, these people appreciating my knives not because of my silver tongue or gimmicky demonstrations but because they *need* the blades. They need to butcher wild game. They need to split open the reddened western sky, rip through the unforgiving landscape, spill the choked, bloodied guts of anything standing between them and their collective fate, our collective fate, Our Manifest Destiny. And just for a moment, as I'm drifting toward the end of this dream, I sense something much bigger than myself, much bigger even than my knives. But then I wake up.

❋

Outside a monolithic arena in Wichita, Kansas, a girl asks me to cut her. It's an hour after the show. The swarms of breathless fans, chests swollen with edged faith, have left the arena. The parking lot is empty. I don't see it coming as she approaches, her face blank, blonde hair lilting in the prairie wind. Preparing to sign a poster or ticket stub, I pull out my pen. But when she reaches me, her hands hang to her thighs, empty.

She asks me to cut her.

I decline. I've never taken the blade to human flesh.

She insists that I cut her. She tells me she's seventeen and she lives in the suburbs, says her father is a surgeon and her mother a homemaker. They've given her a Lexus and a platinum credit card and a waiting college trust — everything she's ever wanted — but they won't cut her. As she speaks, her eyes glint like specks of spilled silver.

I tell her it sounds like her father is qualified to cut her.

She tells me she asked him. He wouldn't do it. Instead, he sent her to a psychiatrist with dyed black hair and a thick lisp. She tells me she wants to be cut just this once, to make sure there's still blood inside.

I take out my Cutcorp pocket knife and open it up. I ask her where she wants it.

She points to a spot on the outside of her arm, just below her shoulder, the place where a roofer might get a tattoo. I move closer. I lift the sleeve of her tee-shirt and press my hand against her skin, imagining the blood vessels beneath my fingers, wondering how deep I need to go. And then, without nervous chatter, without a word, I raise the knife to her arm, the blade pointed at the ground, and press it gently at first, but then harder, into her skin. I run it down her arm. A single gash, three inches long.

The blood rises slowly, red dotting the surface of her arm. But soon blood fills the slit I've carved and pools on her skin, sticky and thick, smelling like iron. She turns her arm inward, leans over her shoulder, and watches as the blood slicks down, drips onto the hot black asphalt.

❈

After two months of traveling, two months spent before sold-out crowds in civic centers and college gymnasiums, I have a two-day break. I go home. We celebrate Jeff's birthday — he turned four two weeks ago, while I was in Sioux Falls, South Dakota.

Sitting at the dining table, I hand Jeff his birthday present. He unwraps the package manically, like its contents might soon disappear. It's a combat knife, Cutcorp's reproduction of the knife his great grandfather carried during World War II. Instinctively, he unsheathes it and stabs it into the piece of chocolate cake in front of him. It's so sharp it cuts through the glass plate down into the mahogany of the dining table, where it lodges. His mother and I clap and coo, proud of his poise. His mother raises the camera, and I slide around the table next to him, our smiles outshined only by the glimmer of the blade. Cheese, we say.

❈

I'm on the tour bus, somewhere north of Chattanooga, riding out the waves of Appalachia that swell before us. The bus is sponsored by the Food Network. It's got a gourmet kitchen and a live-in chef. He's one of Emeril Lagasse's interns, Hillary told me. He doesn't say Bam, but he's the real Cajun deal — I hear swampy bayous every time he opens his mouth. Hillary arranged the whole thing: they get tapes of my shows to air late at night (interspersed with advertisements for Cutcorp, of course); we get the bus and the chef and the box set of the Food Network's greatest bloopers. Hillary sits Indian-style in the floor of the bus's living room, her fingertips caressing an unfolded United States map. She insists I watch the bloopers DVD, says I've been a little bit tense lately, that the bloopers will help me relax. But we're already on the fourth disc, and after awhile kitchen fires and broken dishes and spilled stroganoff begin to lose their charm.

I'm watching a slow motion replay of a guy getting pied when Hillary says, I can't believe it.

Can't believe what, I ask her.

I knew something wasn't right, but I had no idea it was this big, she says.

I don't say anything. If she wants to tell me, she will, I decide. We've been on the road for nearly four months now, and I'm tired of her circumlocution, tired of her leaving me out of things — tour decisions, contract arrangements, advertising deals.

She keeps pointing to a place on the map, her expression goofy, incredulous. I don't like it. I like it even less when she finally speaks. We missed Alabama, she says. I tried booking it before Florida, but there was a scheduling conflict, a college football game. And then I forgot about it completely.

That's a damn shame, I say. I take a bite of the

turducken Emeril's understudy carried back to me earlier. It's excellent, if a bit rich.

A damn shame? Catastrophic is more like it. It's November, Andy, the middle of deer season in a state with two million deer.

I ask her what one state is going to hurt. I remind her how well we've been doing, how unbelievable our sales numbers are.

We've got an open weekend after Richmond. If we drive it straight through, we can go to Alabama, one quick stop, and make it to Baltimore by showtime on Monday.

I'm scheduled to go home that weekend, to spend a couple of days with Jeff and Mandy, but before I can protest, Hillary is on the phone, screaming at the person on the other end, threatening their job, their family, their life, if they don't *just make it happen.*

I take out my phone too. After three rings Mandy answers. Mandy, where are you?

I'm at home filming videos of Jeff. He's dancing.

I say that must be cute.

Not cute enough, she tells me.

I ask her what she means.

She tells me she's been filming him every day for a week, uploading the videos onto YouTube. She says he hasn't even gotten a hundred thousand hits. Says there are babies with millions of hits but our kid is a failure. Jeff is a failure. She blames it all on me. She has excellent rhythm.

I tell her Jeff isn't a baby anymore. He's four years

old, with the motor skills of a kindergartner. I tell her to film Jeff throwing knives at the target I bought for him.

She sighs. But that's not what people want on YouTube. They want babies, dancing babies. Her voice has a frantic, unfamiliar tone.

I decide to tell her the bad news, that I won't be coming home after my show in Richmond, that Hillary's booking a show in Alabama. Then I tell her how tired I am, how badly I want to spend time with her and Jeff, how I'd hoped we could all go to a children's movie, how nice it would be to get our hands sticky with buttery popcorn and watch a bunch of make-believe creatures escape from make-believe trouble.

She asks what's wrong with me, tells me I don't sound like the knife salesman she's always known, the knife salesman she married. She asks me if I want to be mediocre, if I want to be a failure like our son.

❄

The show in Charlotte is over, just finished, the hum of the crowd still singing through the arena's concourses. I follow a tunnel toward the dressing room, toweling blood smears from my face. A man stands down the hallway in front of me, leaning against the wall, his face hidden in a shadow. The roadies have carried off my suitcase, the rest of my knives. I reach to my hip, grasp the handle of my puntilla, just to make sure it's there. I call out before I get to him, tell him I'll talk to reporters in the interview room after I shower.

But then he steps into the middle of the tunnel, his figure silhouetted by dim, winding light. As I get closer I see that he's old, his face wrinkled, his hair silvered. I ask who he is.

I'm Jack McGregor, he says.

He doesn't look the way I pictured him, those afternoon visions that kept me walking door-to-door in the St. Louis heat. We shake hands. His eyes shine flat like polished lead. They're fixed above me, looking over me, it seems. I have so much to tell him, so much to thank him for, so much to ask him.

But before I can say anything, he tells me he appreciates my long service. Whispering, he tells me I've been terminated, I am no longer a Cutcorp representative, I can't use his knives anymore. That's all he says and then he pulls open a door in the tunnel wall, escapes to another hallway, to some place I'll never know.

❈

Hillary waits for me on the tour bus. We had a good run, I say. I'm going to the airport, getting a flight to St. Louis, a flight home.

What're you talking about? You're going to Alabama. You're lucky Cutcorp dropped you. Cutcorp was greedy, uptight. We've inked a deal with Bladesmith.

I say, Bladesmith? I can't work for Bladesmith. I wouldn't trust a Bladesmith to butter my toast.

Who cares about the blades, Andy? The contract's signed. Our end is twenty-five percent of all sales. We're going to have a line of miniature knives for kids, lunch boxes to go along with them. A line of geriatric knives, made especially for nursing homes. A line of knives co-sponsored by a European metal band — the suicide series.

❋

My hotel room in Birmingham smells like old smoke. I lie on the bed, staring at the wall, a floral pattern full of daises and carnations that look like they need water. I haven't recovered from finally meeting Jack McGregor, from getting fired by him. I think about the possible reasons. Sure, Hillary has complained about the conditions in my contract since we first joined forces a few months ago, but there was nothing she could do about it. Right after graduating from the Whet Your Feet program I signed a lifetime deal.

I can't call Mandy. She'll complain about Jeff, talk about YouTube, ask me when we can have another child. I sit up on the bed and look at the phone. It's an old one, a wistful gray color. There's the phone in my pocket. But I don't use it. It doesn't seem substantial enough for the conversation I want to have.

I pick up the bedside phone and dial his number. I know it by heart. The line rings three times before he answers. Hello.

Doc, it's me. It's Andy Mills.

Andy?

I got fired. Jack McGregor fired me in person.

I figured that might be coming, he says.

I listen hard, hoping for nostalgia in his voice, but it's not there, only the rasp of countless cigars.

What're you talking about, Doc? I've done nothing but sell knives. I've followed the service manual all the way. Even rule number 137. I've personally tested every single one of the four million blades I've sold over the last few months.

Andy, where are you?

Birmingham. It's deer season, Doc. You wouldn't believe these people.

Are you near a TV? Turn on the news.

Which channel?

Doesn't matter, Andy. Any channel.

I pick up the remote and press power. The Magnavox comes on with a staticky hum. I flip channels, images flicking away as quickly as they come. On CNN, a black woman with a somber expression sits at a newsdesk, a sea of monitors glowing behind her. She's talking about the most recent outbreak, the Charlotte outbreak, and then the screen cuts to a map of the U.S., with cities all across the country dotted, blinking. The map is titled STABBING SPATES. All the dots are cities along the tour, cities I've sold to. The woman says stabbings are up by 500 percent nationwide, emergency rooms are running out of stitches, people are finding guns discarded in the streets, washed up in drainage ditches, left behind for blades, the latest weapon of choice.

And then the screen flashes to black and white security footage from a Louisville supermarket, two women slashing at each other in the produce section, shredded lettuce littering the aisle. Then a cell phone video of a roadside dispute in Tampa, blood spilling from the gut of a man who failed to signal a lane change. Then a boarded up gun store in Houston, gone out of business. Then a junior high lunchroom, where a kid holding a corndog tells the camera guns are boring, tells the camera Cutcorp forever.

✺

The first couple of shows with Bladesmith don't go very well. Sure, the arenas are full just like always, the fans enthusiastic as ever. They don't care about Cutcorp, I realize. They don't pay fifteen bucks a ticket for the integrity of the blades. Somewhere, I'm not sure exactly when it happened, the show had stopped being about knives, stopped being about crisp slices, stopped being about field dressing the world's mysteries.

Somewhere in the West — it could have been Phoenix or Vegas or Sacramento — the show became a spectacle of the obvious, all pomp and stunt and gore, a pornographic fulfillment of basic sensory cravings. And so my audiences, as they watched blood cascade across polished arena floors, as they listened to the whistling swipes of turkey clippings, the dying grunts of my bovine subjects, as they breathed in the soured, intestinal grit of the animals I butchered, they didn't think about the knife quality. They suffered no apprehensions about the probity of my work, the righteousness of my pursuits.

So as I stand in Baltimore with a Bladesmith, my body washed in the seizured blink of the lights, the vulgar eyes of a pulsing crowd upon me, I might as well

70

be holding a rusty spade, might as well be holding a mail-order steak knife, a flea market sword. It wouldn't matter to them.

I labor my way through the show, do my best to veil the deficiencies of the product I wield. A little extra velocity in my swipes and stabs and the audience can hardly tell that the Bladesmith is a utensil of the blissfully primitive, barely more than a blunt club. It is joyless work. For the first time in my life I am enslaved by my job. I am a pawn of industrial failure, a purveyor of mass-produced mediocrity. As I chop my way through crates of wintertime vegetables, my fatigue surpasses that induced simply by my tool's inadequacy.

Toward the end of the show the chute is opened and the bull, hulking and stupid as all the bulls I murder, ambles to the center of the arena, nonchalantly approaching his death. The crowd quiets as the bull nears me, a collective inhale, silence stirring. I approach him slowly, as I always do, appraising his shape, the curve of his throat. I observe his demeanor. Then I scrub his hide with the tip of my dagger. He smells like all the others I've taken: sweet and thick, like hay and sweat and chemicals.

I press my left hand on the side of the bull's neck, his coat warm beneath my palm, muscles taut under flab. I lift the dagger, preparing to swipe it across his jugular, to jump away from his bucking body, to watch the life be expelled from his insides. But then I look at the knife I'm holding. A Bladesmith. It doesn't seem worthy of this sacrifice, this beast's blood. It doesn't seem worthy of my grip.

And so I let go. The dagger falls to the floor, a dull clank on concrete. The bull stands there. He looks at me as I raise my free hand to his neck, as I feel the life I've left in him. Confusion swirls through the crowd in a culminating whisper. Above it, a drunk tells me to give it hell, tells me to slit that fucker's throat.

But I'm already walking away. I walk through the vegetable carnage, through turkey carcasses scattered like blood-soaked rags. I walk through the tunnel, through the locker room, through rolled-open utility doors. I walk through two blue doors beneath a red exit sign, through the crowd gathered early outside, already waiting for me to sign autographs, waiting for me to cut them. When I don't slow down, when I don't stop, they scream and cuss, shake the chain-link fence that separates us.

The Cajun chef pulls the lever, and the door of the tour bus opens. That was a quick one, he says. I nod and head to the back of the bus. It's messy back there — scattered plates of etouffee, scratched bloopers DVDs, blood-stained laundry strewn everywhere. I lean down beside the bed, grope underneath until I feel the plastic handle. I pull on it and out slides my old Cutcorp suitcase, the one I started with eight years ago, still stocked with the full range of sample knives. I yank it up to my shoulder and hurry to the front of the bus.

On my way out the door, Emeril's underling asks if this is an encore.

I tell him it is, tell him it must be.

By the time I make it to the interstate I've stopped looking behind me. I've stopped looking for Hillary, for angry knife-toting fans. I slow down as I make my way up the ramp. I walk on the shoulder. Cars howl past me on their way to friends' houses, to supermarkets, to soccer games.

At the top of the ramp I can see the sun in front of me. It's buoyed on the horizon, trying not to sink. I keep walking. Cars fly by, pushing noisy air around me. I don't know where I'm going, don't know what I'm doing. But I've got my suitcase and I'm headed west.

Summering

The biggest leak of the summer took place on the ocean floor.
For two days everyone along the Gulf Coast sat before
their TVs watching fire consume the oil rig, smoke
rising into the afternoon sky, heavy and static, hanging
like clouds of asphalt. The catastrophe trumped
everything. Tourists left hang-up clothes in condo
closets. Waiters forgot to refill water glasses. Hotel
maids failed to restock towels.

With the whole balmy apparatus of Florida in
jeopardy, Penter Sullivan spent the afternoon in a
flimsy fold-up chair on the beach. Surrounding him
were families with cameras — mothers and fathers and
sons and daughters, most of them in stark white polos
and pressed khaki shorts. They posed on the sand and
posed in ankle-deep water, snapping photos of the end
of vacation.

Penter wasn't on vacation. He hadn't worked in
months. He was a plumber — a freelancing plumber, he
told himself. He made house calls for his father's
friends, for nosy neighbors who'd heard he'd moved
back to Destin. They'd call him about leaks or clogs,
he'd do a routine fix, make up a price, and scribble
illegibly on carbon copy invoices.

Penter stayed on the beach while the photo shoots
finished up. The sun lowered under an anvil of black
smoke; pink rays bent across the water's surface and

dissolved into the horizon. Finally he folded his chair and carried it across the sand toward his house. He was sunburned and he was hungry, and he'd realized neither until he stood up and moved. As he walked, Penter admired his home, an oceanfront Victorian. It had been his parents' house, but shortly after Penter's mother died, Penter's father, unable to stomach Destin's changing demographic, had purchased a place in nearby Seaside. "Destin used to be a fishing village," he'd told Penter over the phone. "Now I go outside for the Sunday paper and there are kids funneling beer and fondling each other." Making the most of the old man's snobbery, Penter had goaded him with anecdotes of cut-off tee-shirts, chain necklaces, and unkempt goatees. Several months later his father had handed over the keys.

Penter slid open the patio door. His sun-swollen shoulders carried the heat of afternoon into the cool interior, his toes shedding sand onto cold tiles. Allison was on the living room couch, hunched over a laptop. Penter grabbed a green aloe vera bottle from the fridge and sat down next to her. "What're you doing?"

He held the bottle out and she took it.

"You should've worn a higher SPF," she said, without looking away from her screen. She was in hunter green scrubs and white foam shoes that seemed to belong on the feet of an astronaut.

"So you won't do it?"

"When I finish this article."

Penter searched under couch pillows for the remote control. He leaned toward her, trying to look at the laptop, but she closed it.

"The jellyfish are going to be all right," she said, squirting a dollop of aloe vera into her palm. With minimal enthusiasm, she began rubbing his shoulders — the half-bored way she handled her patients, he imagined. But Penter didn't complain.

Finished, she got up and walked to the other side of the coffee table. She stood there, her posture simultaneously grand and terrified. Her hands were shaking. "I have something to show you, Penter. Come with me." Her voice was trembling.

He followed her down the hallway, out the front door. In the driveway, parked beside Penter's truck, was an orange moving van.

"Do you know what that is?" she asked, pointing at the van.

"A U-Haul?" he guessed.

She was still pointing at the van. "That's me leaving you."

"I don't understand."

"It was the pelicans. You didn't even blink when the news showed those pelicans covered in oil. You don't care about anything. Not me. Not yourself. Not even nature."

"No, I don't understand why you need a moving van."

"It's a symbolic gesture, Penter."

"I mean, you don't have that much stuff."

"I hoped it would make you realize some things."
She led him to the back of the van. He watched as she
rolled open the enormous door. Inside the cavernous
box was a single black suitcase.

Penter stared at the suitcase. He turned to her. Her
face was a pale red. He expected her to cry but she
didn't — it somehow made him feel worse. After a long
pause he said, "I hope you didn't pay for the flat tire
insurance."

Penter stood in the yard watching as Allison backed
the beeping van out of the driveway and executed an
eight-point turn. Heading back inside, he found a
cardboard box by the front door. He carried it into the
kitchen, cut through an elaborate network of tape, and
unpacked a spool of blue plastic tubing, thin and coiled
like oversized telephone wire — the Pex pipes he'd
ordered. Though he'd expected the plumbing supplies,
the reality of the opened box disappointed him. The
stack of mail on the counter had the same effect. Fake
checks with dozens of zeros. A bill from his dentist, its
tone strangely apologetic. Another postcard from his
father: "Saw not one but two people wearing Harley
Davidson tee-shirts today. Watched a couple let their
baby play in the ocean in a diaper. Love, Dad."

❈

In the back of the fridge that night, Penter found
Allison's vodka watermelon. The upturned bottle she'd
planted in the rind had drained to infuse the fruit. He
dropped the bottle in the sink and cut the melon in half,

dug out a pink spoonful for taste. The flavor was mostly intact.

In the living room he flipped through the channels. More coverage of the spill — but he wanted to put the greased feathers of pelicans out of mind. He settled on one of the shopping networks. Two women in startling makeup hawked jewelry made of stones that could be dissolved into a calcium-rich beverage. The set surrounding the women was alarmingly white and made the pair seem vaguely angelic. "Never miss your daily dose of calcium again," the woman with turquoise eyeshadow said. "Just remove the pendant and drop it into your water or tea for a tasty and healthful treat." The other woman had beige eyebrows and tapped a bell every time a new order was placed. "Remember to stir briskly."

An hour later Penter had strip-mined the vodka-melon and his cheeks were coated in sugar, fingers sticky with juice. He carried the box of newly delivered pipes downstairs to the guest bedroom, his makeshift plumbing supply closet. He stood amid his equipment taking drunken inventory. A sledgehammer lay on the bed, brass fittings littered the bedside table, caulking tubes were strewn across the floor like abandoned crayons. It was an awful waste, he decided — all those supplies and no leaky pipes, no problem toilets.

He grabbed a wrench from the window seat. In the attached bathroom he flipped open the cabinet beneath the sink, turned the water off at the wall, then locked the wrench onto a slip nut and began twisting. As he wrestled with the fitting, the wrench slipped and smashed his fingers against the pipe. The task was more strenuous than he remembered, hands cramped around the wrench, his forearms aching. He imagined some over-muscled apprentice installing this pipe, someone like his graceless trade school peers.

When the sink trap dropped to the cabinet floor, Penter slumped against the wall and stared at the dismantled fixture, his head resonant with drink. He looked down at his throbbing hands. Blood dripped from a split in the tip of his left thumb, running into his palm and gumming between his fingers. He reached for the hand towel hanging above him and cinched it around the wound, the achy pressure oddly satisfying. On the towel were his embroidered initials. Even the forgotten guestroom items had been subject to Allison's indiscriminate monogramming. Penter had always been baffled by the contrived stateliness of monograms, but he'd never brought it up. Omission — that was his preferred form of romantic expression; that was how he displayed affection.

Penter waited for the bleeding to stop, unwrapping his thumb every few minutes to check it. Once the blood had hardened, he pushed himself up to the sink. He turned the cold knob and held his hands below the faucet, waiting for water that wouldn't come.

❊

The Truesdales called about their pool a few days later, and Penter was excited to have the work. He loaded up his truck and headed over. Their place was only a few blocks inland, on the edge of his neighborhood. It was a low-profile modern bungalow that looked like a sinking houseboat, a hull engulfed in the green of their lawn. Penter knew Mrs. Truesdale as the thin woman who circled the neighborhood in spandex. A woman his mother had privately called a slut.

To most of the neighborhood Penter was a joke — a so-called plumber from a well-off family on perpetual vacation. His father had made a quick fortune in solar-powered radios, and the Sullivans had moved to Florida and watched as their investments thrived amidst the technological bewilderment of the nineties. After high school, when most of Penter's friends headed off to private colleges under scholarships with odd, vaguely criminal surnames attached, Penter enrolled at a modest public university, the sort of place where student and professor alike were in a hurry to leave. He'd never even considered the path of his classmates. Never, not even for a moment, did he think about donning a cheap, itchy suit to interview for lowly banking positions; never contemplated subjecting himself to law school. Instead he dropped out and switched to vocational school, his career choice an act of rebellion, a prank on his father that now, seven years later, was still in progress.

Penter knocked on the Truesdales' door and waited. A dog yipped. Footsteps. And then Mrs. Truesdale appeared. She looked to be in her late fifties, still very thin and still sporting spandex. She wore her silver hair combed straight back in a way that emphasized a substantial forehead.

Before Penter could introduce himself she launched into an exhaustive history of the leak: the confusion over which pool company to hire, the style restrictions from the neighborhood association, difficulties accessing the property's main plumbing line, her husband's general ineptitude

"Why are you still standing outside?" she asked.

"I'm just listening."

"Well, come in. Ed will want to speak with you. He's clueless about these things but that doesn't stop him talking about them."

The air in the house smelled like antique furniture, oily and dusty both. Penter followed her down a wide hallway to a den, where a pair of low recliners slouched side by side. A skinny old man sat in one watching television. Onscreen, two enormous men with exotically tan skin and ornate tattoos gripped each other on the floor of an octagonal ring, a referee standing nearby, cheeks fat and whistle-flexed.

Mrs. Truesdale sneaked up to the chair and slapped the old man's arm. "Ed, the plumber's here."

"Could you get the door, Katherine?" He pointed to the screen. "Jones is about to do his achilles lock."

"I already answered it. He's right here." She motioned to Penter.

The man sprang from his chair, surprisingly spry. He looked to be about a decade older than Katherine. He wore a tight black tee-shirt decorated with an intricate iron-on design — fine white lines criss-crossing wildly from his abdomen to his ribcage. Above them, in the center of his sunken chest, was the word TAPOUT. On his head he wore a stiff wool cap, its bill long and flat, twisted to the side. It was the garb of a teenage boy, the sort of dirty-looking kid Penter might encounter at the movie theater.

Ed stuck out his hand, dark with the pigmentation of aged beef and callused, bony. "Ed Truesdale," he said. "Appreciate you coming over. I'll pause my fight and we'll go have a look at the pool." He held the remote control up to his face, squinting.

"You don't have to miss the big fight, Ed," Penter said, his voice loud and strangely parental in his own ears. "I bet I could handle it."

"Nah, I'm just reviewing this fight. It's from July of last year. It ends at the 2:38 mark of the next round, guillotine choke to tapout." He opened a glass door that led to a poolside patio. "Pool's right out here."

The pool's hardware was tucked between two ferny hedges. Penter found the leak right away, in the corroded coupling connected to the pool's filter. He examined the part and mumbled numbers to himself, heading out to search his supplies in the truck. He returned with toolbox in one hand and new coupling in the other. Ed was still standing outside.

"Had to dig around," Penter said, holding out the coupling. "But this one should fit."

He walked over to the filter, crouched, and began the tedious work of removing the old coupling, straining to turn the pipe wrench, mud caking around his feet. Ed stood over him, watching.

"So you're an Ultimate Fighting fan, huh?" asked Penter.

"I'm not just any old fan. I'm big into the local scene."

Penter stopped turning his wrench. "Destin has a fighting scene? Seems too laid back for that."

"Maybe your version of Destin. But I grew up on the docks in the fifties and sixties, when men fought about fish all the time. It was a real macho thing — more than once I saw one man bust another man's nose over fishing territory. Anyway, the guys fight in this junior-high gym over in the poor part of town. I work outta there as a promoter."

"What exactly does being a promoter entail?" The old coupling came off and Penter began connecting the new one.

Ed frowned like Penter's ignorance disappointed him. "Promoting, mostly. I make posters, record radio ads, maybe the occasional latenight TV spot. I get my pick of the best fighters because I interpret the term *promotion* loosely."

Penter was tightening a series of nuts.

"What I'm saying is, I'm also into intimidation. Anything to get my fighter a psychological advantage over his opponent."

If Ed was joking, Penter couldn't tell. "Intimidation?"

"Well, here's an example. There's a big fight coming

up in a few weeks. My guy's Rabid Richey Zercutto. He's fighting this fucking punk, a cashier at that hamburger place out on highway nine. Jerry's. I've been going out there about twice a week just to mess with his head. I use my AARP card to get discount burgers, and I'll take one burger apart, make a real mess of it, smear greasy lettuce and tomato and mayo all over my tray, and then I take it back up to him and scowl at him while he's cleaning it up."

Penter laughed, again unable to tell if Ed was serious. He'd always had that problem with old people — his grandmother could tell a fart joke and look like John Wayne squinting into the wind.

"You could join me sometime. I normally order two and eat one of 'em."

"I don't think I'd eat any of those burgers if I were you."

✳

The next afternoon Penter sat on the couch watching a reality show about washed-up sitcom actors living under the conditions of their former roles. There was a long segment on the woman who'd played Kimmy Gibbler — it followed her move to San Francisco, her investment in a drawer-full of headbands and dangly earrings, and her utilization of strange facial expressions. Thinking that the show's producers had played loose and fast with their own premise, Penter turned it off.

He pulled out his cell and dialed his father's number, but no one answered. A few minutes later, the house phone rang. Penter walked to the kitchen to answer it.

"Hello, is this Penter?"

"This is he."

"Yes, Ed and I were talking earlier and realized we've got some more questions about the pool. Is there any way we could schedule another appointment?"

"Of course."

"When would you be able to come back?"

"Actually, what're y'all up to right now?"

An hour later, Penter sat on the Truesdales' patio, a stein of beer in hand, its icy condensation dripping on his sunburned knees. They had drawn the lawn chairs up to the pool, their backs to the sun, but a breezy darkness had long since fallen.

When he'd first arrived, they'd asked him a few questions about the condition of the rest of their pool's plumbing. He examined the chlorine generator, knocked on a few pipes, and said, "I'm no pool expert, but the future looks pretty scary. The pipes are already corroding and the generator is making a funny noise."

"That's what I've been telling her," said Ed. "That generator's as old as those two holes in the sky in New York City. The day after those towers fell, I had the pool company come out here."

Penter couldn't tell if those two occurrences were somehow related. He was about to ask when Katherine said, "It's amazing it's lasted so long, with Ed pouring in twice as much salt as he's supposed to."

"I like a salty pool. Like the way it makes my skin feel. Those numbers are just recommendations. Some scientists in a lab somewhere came up with them."

Katherine said, "That's my point, Ed. Scientists came up with them."

"Well, what kind of scientists devote themselves to the study of pools, huh? Now that's the real issue here."

After several beers, Penter's skin was coated with an inebriated glow, a tingling sensitivity to the considerable loveliness of the Truesdales's backyard, their salty swimming pool, and even the Truesdales themselves. Penter listened as they argued about who to invite to their pool party.

"I'm not inviting Darren. I don't care if he is our son, Katherine. He's square. A regular four by four. He and his wife just sit around and scowl. And that baby, it'll shit and scream all over the place."

"That baby is our grandson," Katherine said, smiling at Penter.

Ed got up to light a few of the tiki torches lining the patio. Katherine turned to Penter. "You'll be attending, won't you?"

"My schedule's very busy."

"Don't be ridiculous. You'll be the star of the party — the plumber who saved the pool."

At that she stood up and pulled her shoulders out from under the straps of her dress, and it dropped to the concrete. She unsnapped her bra, peeled down her modest cotton panties, and tiptoed toward the diving board, the same proud gait that had been circling the neighborhood for decades. In the soft, shaky light of the tiki torches, Katherine looked, somehow, both older and more beautiful than she did with clothes on. As she stood on the diving board, her pale body seemed essential to the languid physics of nighttime, the push and pull of stars overhead.

Or maybe Penter was simply drunk.

He looked at Ed. A spellbound grin had formed on the old guy's face. Katherine dove and her body disappeared beneath a beaded spray. Ed turned to Penter. "I think you and I both have better manners than we've displayed here tonight." He stood and Penter did too, preparing to leave. But then Ed pulled his shirt off, ripped his pants down, and hopped out over the water, clutching his bony legs to his chest in cannonball form. An unimpressive splash misted Penter's shins.

Bobbing back up, Ed called: "What're you waiting for, Penter? We promise not to stare at your wine cork." Katherine kept on swimming; her silence made Ed's request more forceful.

Penter began undressing slowly, but his pace increased with each item he removed. By the time he tripped out of his underwear, they were treading water beneath the diving board, pretending not to watch as he dove in.

❈

Climbing into bed that night, Penter turned on the television and flipped channels until he came to the oil leak. There were bemused voice-overs discussing the projected number of barrels spilled. They were showing aerial panoramas of the ocean, and Penter thought there was beauty in the oil's cloudy distillation, the way it veined across the water's surface, in the windswept swirl of the larger plumes. Just before he fell asleep, he decided the oil was headed to Destin and there was not a goddamn thing anyone could do. And in a dreamy, exhausted way, that thought pleased him.

❄

At the Truesdales' party Penter stood near the pool, admiring the strange mix of people. Grouped around Katherine were the young women she taught at the aerobics studio. They sported frizzy ponytails and neon colors — so devoted to the fashions of their childhood that they followed the era's fitness trends. Ed was surrounded by a group of UFC acquaintances. One of them had to be Rabid Richey, but to the untrained eye they all looked the same. They wore baggy shorts with too many pockets, tight tee-shirts with flamboyant designs, and wide-framed sunglasses, which they left on long after the sun sank, its rays diffuse between the sagging leaves of the palms.

The pool was the party's centerpiece. The water churned with the arm flaps of unclaimed children, bubbled with the concentric turbulence of cannonballs. In the shallow end, a balding man held a baby above the splashing, insisting that the other children calm down. "No running," he repeated. "Perhaps we should institute a limit on stunt splashing — everyone gets one cannonball, one jackknife, and one can opener."

Every now and then, Ed or Katherine would point to Penter and then point to the pool, and the people to whom they spoke would turn to stare at the pool as they listened, like maybe the blue on its surface would shiver into some meaningful formation, some profound shape. But it was just a swimming pool.

Penter drank beer so fast his eyes ached from the cold. He spent the evening nodding, carefully maneuvering between conversations about submission holds and others about the genius of Brat Pack films, the speakers and listeners participating with zest, the brief but focused interactions of which good parties are made.

It was late in the evening when he found Katherine slumped on the ground next to the keg, its plastic spout in her hand.

"Would you give me a pump?" she asked.

Penter pressed the pump up and down until it firmed. She raised the spout to her mouth and sprayed, her cheeks distended as she gulped. She offered it to Penter but he refused, pointing to the can in his hand.

"What's up?" he asked.

"I wanted a Volkswagen," she said. "Ed said the resale value would be too low. People hate Germans, he said."

"When was this?"

"Almost forty years ago, just after we married."

"You're still upset?" He leaned toward her with his mouth open. She raised the spout and held it over his wide lips. The beer was airy, exhausted fizz.

"You learn to live with such tragedies but they never go away. I kept thinking, at some point I will grow up. At some point I'll stop wanting stupid things. But forty years later I'm a grandmother and I'm still considering the lost possibilities of a German coupe."

"At least there's something you want. I spend a lot of my time on the internet, writing angry comments below local news stories. Sometimes I try to talk people into better plumbing equipment, but most don't listen."

She grabbed his hand. They were moving now, across the lawn, squeezing between patio chairs in which barely conscious people slouched. Penter had no idea where they were going. As she pulled him, she said, "Ed wants his fighter to beat up a cashier — that thought makes him happy. Sometimes when we're lying in bed he'll turn toward me and say: 'Do you know how much of my life I've spent waiting in lines to pay? This beating is for all of them, all of the slow cashiers.'"

"I think that's just his way of getting psyched up."

"Maybe. And then his fighter will probably lose and Ed will pout for a month. But then he'll just start wanting someone else to get beat up."

Inside the house Ed was giving his UFC buddies a tour. As he and Katherine passed them, Penter overheard Ed explaining the kitchen renovation, his brawny friends looking up at the track lighting, rubbing their hands across the granite countertops.

Katherine leaned on him as they walked upstairs, her arm wrapped in his. Her body seemed limber, free from the stiffness of age. Penter was taken with the graceful-ness of her inebriation, thinking that maybe he should start aerobics.

Upstairs, she led him past doors marked with various

oceanic symbols. He stopped, pointed to a starfish. "What are these markers for?"

"Oh, that's the motif of the room. That particular room celebrates the quiet existence of the starfish."

"So the entire room is dedicated to starfish?"

"There are over eighteen hundred species of starfish."

"Can I see it?"

"It's a mess right now. Or as Ed says, the ecosystem is disturbed by our laundry."

At the end of the hall they stopped before a door with a crooked seahorse hanging next to it.

"You wanted to show me the seahorse room?" Penter asked.

She opened the door and flipped on the light. The space was full of blue marlins. Two stuffed marlins lay side-by-side on the bed, their stiff bodies clinging to stained slabs of wood. Grainy black and white photos lined the walls: cigar-mouthed men gathered around a marlin; a row of needle-billed fish laid across the floor of a boat; a man standing on the dock with a large, fish-shaped trophy in his hands. In the corner of the room was a messy bouquet of fishing poles, their fiberglass bowing between ceiling and floor.

"Is this the Ernest Hemingway room?" Penter asked.

"It's my father's room. Or filled with his stuff any-way — he never stepped foot in it. He ran a charter fishing boat, the best marlin outfit on the Gulf."

Penter carefully took a lure from a shelf on the wall, a contraption with two dangling discs, chartreuse bands of rubber, and a cartoonishly big hook. "This stuff is incredible."

"Dad was an asshole — he spent all of his time out on the ocean with drunk businessmen and giddy honeymooners. Everyone loved him and my mom and I hated him for it." She pointed to one of the mounted fish. "That was all he ever wanted: marlins."

"Why have you kept all this stuff?"

"I'd consider getting rid of it. Selling it, or maybe donating it to a museum or something. But it's because of all this I met Ed."

Penter sat down on the bed next to the stuffed fish, and Katherine sat beside him. He said, "Yeah. Ed mentioned growing up on the docks."

"His father was a trash fisherman — that's what my dad called anyone who didn't fish for bill fish. Our fathers hated each other. When he was about eighteen, Ed got on with my father's boat. I think Ed and my dad agreed to it just to spite Ed's father. Anyway, Ed picked marlins and he picked me. I always thought it was romantic, like we were the Romeo and Juliet of Destin, Florida."

Penter picked up a heavy brass fishing reel, cradling it in his hand like a supermarket fruit. "Why'd you show me this stuff?"

"Because I wanted you to see it," she said.

※

In the days following the party, Penter spent more and more time at the Truesdales' house, devoting all his professional attention to their pool. Because he didn't want to limit their pool access, Penter replaced its decaying equipment slowly, the Truesdales approving every repair he suggested. By the end of July, he'd completed something close to a full renovation. He'd restored the main drains and skimmers, updated the corroded pump and repaired its long-failing vacuum port. The pool operated with remarkable efficiency, its pristine surface glinting with a blue of unprecedented depth and vitality.

Penter's relationship with the Truesdales wasn't all business. He often spent mornings at Ed's gym, where they watched burly men jumping rope, bruising their knuckles on punching bags, and gulping protein shakes from squirt bottles. They watched Rabid Richey spar, each blow of his fist misting the air with sweat. And while Ed took his afternoon naps, Penter would spend long hours in the pool with Katherine, sunbathing on flimsy inflatable rafts, sipping frothy alcoholic concoctions poured from her blender. Together with the Truesdales, he regularly turned the gray of evening into the dotted black of midnight out by the pool, the radio tuned to hits from Ed's high school days, the music's crooning sentimentality novel, if not poignant.

Ed and Katherine introduced Penter to an entirely new plumbing market. Ed posted flyers for Penter's services at the MMA gym, and Katherine announced his availability to her crowded aerobics classes. Soon Penter was getting phone calls from people who had never been in a golf foursome with his father, never played bridge with his mother.

And it wasn't long before Penter was spending the night at the Truesdales' place, his reasons increasingly ridiculous: late-night excuses about being locked out of his house, about proximity to the hardware store, about the coarseness of his bed sheets at home. But Ed and Katherine weren't concerned. Once or twice, Penter brought up the subject of how much time he was spending at their house, but they wouldn't hear it. Ed said, "Shit, Penter. You're our plumber. You're taking care of our pool. Far as I'm concerned, that means 'mi casa es su casa.'"

At the breakfast table one morning, he told Katherine he didn't know what was wrong with him but he didn't want to go home.

"Honey, you're summering. People do it all across the coast every year."

"Yeah, but they're from Tennessee. Kentucky, maybe. I live two blocks away."

"Doesn't make any difference. Stop dwelling on minor distinctions."

And that night, as he readied himself for bed in the Starfish Room, he realized she was right: he was summering. Taking a vacation from the disapproval of the women he'd dated. From his father's snobby postcards. From the faint, obligatory grief he felt over his mother's death. But still Penter wondered when he'd return to his life, wondered if he had much of a life to return to. All of Penter's relationships — romantic and familial and platonic — had been characterized by an elaborate progression of mutual disappointments. But with the Truesdales things were different. With the Truesdales he'd found companionship free from the usual rules, the usual expectations.

His bed in the Starfish Room was much smaller than his bed at home, but he liked the way his body filled the space. On the ceiling were painted starfish by the dozens, celestial in color and arrangement. At night Penter lay squinting up at them, trying to determine their shape, their order, but the darkness made them seem squirmy, restless.

✺

Penter had been called to the pier to fix a broken toilet on a yacht, but he decided to stick around afterwards. It was his first time visiting the docks since high school. He walked past restaurants that opened to the water-front, their insides green with tacked-up dollar bills, lacy bras drooping from their rafters like Spanish moss. Unseen speakers blared songs with choruses about salty beers and weekend pirates. It was a charade of maritime culture.

In the harbor were new boats, polished white, hulls glistening. Aboard them stood trim men in tucked-in shirts, cell phones on their belts. They looked more like car salesmen than people who made a life pulling fish from the sea. Penter walked past these boats, past the flip-flop patter of tank-topped tourists, all the way to the pier's end, where he found a row of old boats slumping in the water, algae browning their sides, rails hung with duct-taped buoys. Onboard, tattooed men hefted slick fish, hanging them on wooden peg boards like marketplace sausages.

Motoring slowly toward the harbor was a rust-eaten boat, a scrawny figure manning the wheel, guiding it into a slip. The driver was tying up to the dock when Penter approached and saw he was a teenager, a boy with wispy bangs and sunglasses dangling from his neck on a neoprene lanyard. He was whipping rope up from the water, wrapping it around his elbow, and gusts of hot wind were inflating his nylon shirt like a sail — it seemed that he might levitate from the deck of the boat, ascend into the afternoon. When he noticed Penter, he tossed the rope aside, his posture stiffening.

"Are you a fisherman?" asked Penter.

"Yeah. But I don't take clients."

"Where's the captain?"

The boy examined Penter closely and then looked around at the other boats. "You're not with Fish and Wildlife, are you?"

"No."

"Coast Guard?"

"Listen, I'm affiliated with zero government agencies. I'd just like to speak to whoever's in charge here."

The boy motioned Penter aboard. Penter walked to the back of the boat and climbed in. The floor was slick with briny-smelling slime. The boy pulled out a cigarette, lit it with his back to the wind, and took a long, squinty drag. Exhaling, he said, "Boat's registered to my dad, but I'm the de facto captain."

"De facto captain?"

"That's me."

"You know what that means?"

"My social studies teacher says it all the time."

"Where's your father?"

The boy picked up a hose and began spraying the boat floor, stirring up the pungent fish odor. "I'm the captain, like I said. And I'm not gonna take you and your old fraternity buddies fishing. I'm not out here to bait the hook of every idiot tourist from Detroit."

"I grew up here and I don't want to go fishing. I just want a fish."

"You seem kind of clueless for a local." The boy's face slackened, the defensive creases disappearing from the edge of his eyes.

"Yeah, I was born here but I've always felt like a tourist — I never understood the point of drag racing and my skin gets wrinkled in the ocean."

"Kind of fish you want?"

"A blue marlin. You ever catch 'em?"

"When I want to. That's not very often. You don't need a marlin."

"Why not?"

"No one needs a marlin — they're unsanitary. They spend half their time swimming around Miami sewers."

Penter thought for a moment, looking out at the ocean. Under a graying sky the water glistened blue, its surface shivering with the afternoon's leftover heat, leftover color. He finally said, "It's not for me. I'll pay you handsomely."

The boy rinsed his hands under the hose. "Well, might take me a while to come across one but if you're willing to pay me *handsomely* I can find you a marlin. We'd need to work out a payment plan."

"I was thinking lump sum but I'm open to other options."

The boy stubbed out his cigarette against the fiberglass side of the boat and tossed it into the water. It floated under the dock. "You're twenty-one years of age, right?"

※

It was the middle of the summer when the oil arrived in Destin. Penter and Ed and Katherine went to see it, walking all the way across the hot beach until the sand sloped toward the ocean. You had to look closely to notice — dotted rows of black across the white beach, stamped into the sand like ink on a page.

"It's just awful," said Katherine. "Just awful." Her words seemed to reveal a determination to be shocked.

"I don't see any oil," said Ed. "That's not what oil looks like where I come from."

"You're from here, Ed," said Katherine.

Penter stood watching the cleanup crews that were stirring along the shoreline. For nearly two months he'd been awaiting the oil's arrival, imagining all the horrible possibilities. He'd felt sure the oil was something important, something big and inevitable that would indelibly change the way people thought about the Gulf Coast, about vacation. For decades people had traveled to Florida in manic pursuit of leisure, and over time Destin — and a thousand similar places — had evolved to serve their notions of happiness and fulfillment. This was the Florida Penter knew — growing up with parents who'd bought into these postcard pleasures: toes in the sand, long rounds of golf, slurred sing-alongs with ambling acoustic guitar solos. Penter had spent weeks wondering if the oil might threaten this Florida, if it might incite some movement to save him from his exceedingly comfortable existence, but now there were people in green shirts ambling along with fishnets, laughing as they scooped up tar balls.

❈

Penter parked his truck in front of the Truesdales' house. He got out and surveyed the street. The neighborhood clicked with sprinklers, their mist giving shape and depth to the air. He opened the tailgate and pulled out a white cooler, his body stiffening as he lowered it to the pavement. He dragged the cooler through the Truesdales' yard toward the back patio, leaving a trail of matted grass. There was no time to pick it up, to ring the doorbell for help.

On the patio, he opened the lid. In a foot of water lay a blue marlin, its bill wedged against the cooler wall, its body curled in swimming pose, tail cocked and ready to flap. The belly convulsed as the gills flexed for oxygen, fins thrumming against plastic. The blue of the fish seemed to tint the water with a delicate glow.

Penter dipped his hands into the water, touching the fish for the first time. Its stomach, when he wrapped his fingers under it, felt both slimy and smooth, firm but elastic. He gripped and lifted, and for a moment he held the marlin. It was strangely compliant, strangely still, in his hands. Its fins curved up at sharp angles, needled bill pointing forward. Out of the water, the marlin changed colors, darkening somehow in the sunlight. The teenage fisherman had said it was just a baby, a yearling he'd guessed, but standing there in the afternoon, with the fish poised in his hands like a trophy, Penter thought it looked ancient, like something molded and hardened in the ocean's cold blue deep, something borne of the blind forever that preceded the warm, oily dream of Florida.

It occurred to Penter then that what he held was a fish struggling to survive in the heat of the afternoon. He had to get it in the water. Cradling the marlin against his body, Penter shuffled to the pool's edge and tossed the fish. It slapped the surface, graceless and stunned, and for a moment lay there, a pectoral fin circling listlessly, gills spilling wheezy slurps.

Penter watched as it drifted, pulled by the undercurrent of the intake valve, toward the stiff current of the pool's main jet. The fins gained traction, gills flushing the salty water, and in an instant the marlin submerged and darted in a wink of silver across the deep end. Just before its bill could smash into the wall, it glided into a slow lap of the pool's perimeter.

Relieved, Penter went to find Ed and Katherine. The patio door was locked. He shook the handle, then knocked loudly. Mrs. Truesdale answered, a tiny dumbbell in one hand, a melting popsicle in the other.

"What're you doing, Penter?"

"Where's Ed?"

Penter followed her into the den, where Ed was watching television. It was a reality show on MTV — tattooed teenagers screaming at one another. When Ed saw Penter, he said, "Jenny screwed Myles but Will doesn't know it yet."

By the time Penter returned with the Truesdales to the backyard, an afternoon moon hovered overhead, faint as a fingerprint. Together, they peered over the pool's edge. In the center of the deep end, near the bottom, was the marlin. The fish was suspended, a jagged shadow swollen beneath it. They watched in silence, waiting for motion.

"It's a marlin," said Penter. "A gift."

"Where'd you get it?" Katherine asked.

"I made some arrangements with this kid at the pier."

"That thing's not gonna last in the pool, Penter," Ed said.

"It's saltwater," Penter said.

Ed laughed, shaking his head slowly.

They stood studying the fish for a long, quiet minute. Ed seemed annoyed. His mouth was cocked open at a strange angle, revealing a chipped tooth Penter had never noticed. Katherine, on the other hand, leaned toward the pool, smiling. "It's beautiful, Penter," she finally said.

Ed said, "Katherine, you don't want to get too close to this. They're vicious, you know."

She ignored him. "I think Penter's gift calls for some champagne or, at the very least, some daiquiris." She headed back into the house.

When she was gone, Ed leaned toward Penter. "I don't know what to make of this. That fish can't stay here."

"I just thought it might be fun for y'all to have it in the pool a while."

"Fun," said Ed. "Here we've got a regular county fair goldfish, Penter. A real souvenir."

Now the marlin was swimming in small circles. "What's it doing, Ed?"

"Charting its territory, looks like. They're hunters."

Katherine came back with a pitcher of red slush. She poured three cups, handing one to Penter and one to Ed. "Look at it swim," she said. "This is the first time I can remember seeing one alive."

As the day drew dark, Katherine flipped a switch on the side of their house and brittle light flicked into the swimming pool, coloring the water's surface with yellow shapes, a refracted geometry. They drank three pitchers of Katherine's daiquiris and the night eased toward routine, the swimming marlin an afterthought. Ed tuned the radio and hummed along to "Walk Like a Man." Katherine was telling a story about a woman's leotard busting in the middle of her aerobics class when Penter looked over and noticed the fish rising to the surface, fins turning slowly, heavily.

"Shit. I knew this would happen, Penter," said Ed as it floated up on its side, gut ballooning, contracting.

"Calm down, Ed," said Katherine.

"I thought it'd be okay in there — the water's so salty."

Ed glared. "You really thought a marlin would be okay in a swimming pool?"

"I was gonna take it back. Maybe I should take it back now."

"It's too late for that. Damn thing's a goner."

It was still breathing, but in a slow, labored manner. Katherine's demeanor changed as she stared at the dying fish. She was squinting in a way Penter recognized, her cheeks lifted to prevent tears from spilling down them.

Penter walked over to the privacy fence and grabbed a pool skimmer. Standing on the edge of the pool, he reached out with the skimmer and lifted the fish from the surface. It flopped off the net as he tried to swing it over the concrete. He scooped again, guiding it slowly to the patio. The three of them gathered around the marlin, bending down to examine it.

"What're you doing?" asked Ed.

"Trying to see if it's alive," said Penter. "I'm going to take it back."

"I think I can barely hear its gills," Katherine said. She bent closer. The marlin flopped against her legs, and as Katherine jumped back, its bill sliced deep into her calf. She stood there, stunned, as blood streaked to her feet. Penter moved toward her, kneeling to look at the cut. Her skin was open to the muscle, but he couldn't tell if it went any deeper.

Then Katherine was screaming, "Calm down, Ed!

Goddammit, calm down!"

Penter turned to see Ed stomping on the marlin's head, bones and tendons crunching beneath his tennis shoes. When he'd mashed it ragged, he kicked the carcass into the water. Blood plumed.

"Shit. I've made a mess in the pool," he said.

"Because of that temper," said Katherine. "You're an old man with a temper like a teenage boy."

"Let's go to the emergency room," he said, his nostrils whistling as he caught his breath.

"It's not even that deep, Ed. It doesn't even hurt."

"Katherine, I've seen this before. They can get infected. We're going to the emergency room." He grabbed her arm and pulled her. She limped as they moved toward the yard's side gate. Before they reached it, Ed turned and said, "Penter, clean this mess up and go home."

Penter stood there beside the pool. The radio was still playing, another sappy song about cruel parents, about a dead lover. Overhead an airplane blinked red, the flash of light getting smaller and dimmer as it moved away from Destin. Penter kicked off his flip-flops, pulled his shirt over his head, and walked to the pool's shallow end, where the marlin carcass was floating. He tiptoed down the steps into the water, stopping next to the fish. Even with a crushed head, the eyes shone flat like black wax, and the scales gleamed under the blood-tinted water. Penter leaned forward, his feet lifting from the sandpapery floor. He pushed his face into the water, extended his arms above his head, and floated next to the dead marlin. He wanted to sink, to be absorbed, but the salt-dense water pressed him up.

Atlantic Blue

✳

Celia's Aunt Lucille insisted on delivering the gift a week
before the baby shower — she said that would keep our
cousins from getting jealous. And so, on an otherwise
quiet Saturday, we arranged for Lucille to come over.
Before she arrived I sat restlessly in the living room
as Celia tidied up around me. There were little knots on
her temples, her head pregnant with thought.

I asked what she was thinking about.

"I'm wondering if I should have gone to medical
school," she said.

Sometimes it was medical school, other times law.

"The studio's doing fine," I said. "We're doing fine."

"I don't want to take portraits forever," she said.

Without a knock, Aunt Lucille came through the
door. Her arms cradled a neatly wrapped gift.

I punched off the television, and Celia hugged her
aunt around the gift.

"I hardly notice your belly," said Aunt Lucille. She's
one of those family members who speaks in accusations
— maybe Celia was faking the pregnancy for unsoli-
cited gifts.

"I promise it's there," Celia said, as politely as she
could.

I took the gift from Lucille — heavier than it looked
— and hugged her with my free arm. She smelled like
vegetable soup, bland but warm. Ever since Harold

passed, she'd been giving more robust hugs, muscled clasps that lasted, somehow, after she let go.

The three of us settled in the living room, and I held onto the gift. The wrapping paper was immaculate, crisp lines and sharp corners, its perfection unnerving. My own family had a history of wrapping gifts in scraps of newspaper or inside the knotted plastic of supermarket bags. This formal package, the stiffness in Aunt Lucille's shoulders — I could hardly bear them.

I passed the gift to Celia, my hands fumbling, somehow, in the easy exchange. She unthreaded the ribbon with wonderful grace, her thin fingers precise as a pair of Fiskars. And the paper — how she plucked it open and then folded it over, like a seamstress handling fine fabrics. What remained was a box of simple white cardboard, the kind you might find undershirts wrapped in.

She flipped open the flaps and lifted out a delicate contraption. It was a baby mobile, its tin pieces shaped and painted to look like birds in flight — ducks and cranes and pelicans.

"It was your grandfather's," Lucille said. "I've finally accepted that Blair isn't going to have any kids."

Celia studied the mobile with a certain grave appreciation. "The colors are fantastic," she said.

"It's hand-painted," Lucille said. "All original."

I tried to imagine Celia's brawny, bigoted grandfather ever lying beneath such a dainty apparatus.

"It's a beautiful piece," I said, and it was — but even then the mobile felt like an omen, like it had significance I couldn't understand.

❁

Celia's ultrasound was a few weeks later. She lay on the hospital bed and I sat beside her, swiping through photos from our morning shoot with the Silver Sneakers, a geriatric aerobics troupe. Celia's shots were off again — the grins raw-gummed and denture-glinted. During art school, she'd been the best in our class, but she'd grown tired of the business — tired of the chalky lighting, the sleep-starved mothers in wrinkled blouses, the work-stricken fathers with unkempt beards.

I, on the other hand, was born for sad subject matter. My photos made the Silver Sneakers look a dozen years younger. I caught them with their widest smiles, just before cheeks flared into wrinkles, their bulbous hairdos casting stark silhouettes.

Our photo viewing was interrupted when a skinny woman in baggy scrubs entered the room. She introduced herself as the radiology tech and, without saying more, smeared jelly over the small lump of Celia's stomach, the skin stretched to translucence, veins purpling beneath the surface. The woman rubbed the transducer in circles, pressing against the upturned bowl that was our baby's home. Every once in a while she'd stop to examine the screen, her thin body tensing, face shining in the gray light of the monitor.

After a minute-long silence, she said, "Your baby is a fish."

"Excuse me?" I said.

She turned the monitor toward us. A tiny shape was floating in the silver glow of the screen. I could see the arced hump of a dorsal fin, the prominent bulge of eyes. It looked like a minnow.

"Is it healthy?" Celia asked.

She'd heard the tech, she was looking at the same monitor I was, and this was the first thing she'd said.

"I don't know very much about fish," said the tech.

She called in a doctor. Within a few hours the doctor had called in a biologist and a pet store owner. Everyone gathered around the screen, studying it quietly. Finally the pet store owner announced that our fish was female.

The biologist confirmed this assessment. The doctor nodded in a distracted way.

"Is this fairly common?" I asked, uncertain about whom to address. And then, for fear my question hadn't been understood: "A fish daughter, I mean?"

Celia squeezed my tricep, her preferred manner of indicating that I'd committed a faux pas obvious enough to recognize on my own.

"It's hard to say," the biologist said. "Inconsistent reporting."

"I think I remember reading a case study in medical school," the doctor said.

All three of them — the doctor, biologist, pet store owner — agreed that Celia had developed a suitable habitat, a body of water in which our daughter was thriving.

"I wouldn't spend time around any hungry cats," the

pet store owner said.

We laughed, but his face remained sober, his eyes wet like he was allergic to something.

※

Celia and I had always reacted to the world's absurdity with a kind of deadpan stare, as though we were somehow separate from it, as though we were safe. There was, it seemed, a security in our stoicism, in the way we pretended that nothing — not even a fish pregnancy — could disturb our perfectly pleasant lives.

Wasn't that precisely how we'd ended up with a portrait studio inside a big-box retailer? A novel idea, during those listless days after art school, that neither of us was willing to rule out. Neither of us willing to admit we'd be bothered by the ugly commercial setting, by snapping photos of grimacing, third-shift lives. Would we ever have done it if we hadn't thought that somehow — with our middle-class upbringings, our overpriced educations — we were above it all? More than plain snobbery or pretension — this was an aesthetic conviction. A sensibility, developed and deployed to steel us against ugliness and pain.

And it is striking, as I look back, how quickly our convictions turned into everyday truths. Once the novelty thinned we were two people taking portraits for a living. Six years passed, and we were still shooting photos for customers to send to distant relatives.

So when we learned that our daughter was a fish we reacted in our usual manner. We practiced aggressive indifference, even as I accompanied Celia to biweekly appointments with a team of medical and marine professionals, even as they prodded her stomach, guessed at the gestation period, speculated about the species.

Perhaps our sincerest acknowledgement of the circumstances occurred when, during one of our regular trips for ice cream, I suggested our fish was a species sought by anglers of the rougher sort, by rednecks.

Celia drew her face into a look of disgust.

"Would you still love her if she were a largemouth?" I asked.

"I grew up in Alabama," she said. "They were on everyone's wall. People caught them on TV."

We maintained these poker faces even as the pregnancy progressed. One afternoon during the hot middle of July, Celia and I decided to cook out. She sat in the shade of a flimsy awning, drinking tall glasses of ice water from a sweat-specked pitcher. I stood beside her arranging charcoal briquettes with the patience, the skill, of an architect.

"Can't you just light it?" Celia asked. "I'm really hungry."

"The pyramid is everything when it comes to maximizing flame exposure," I said.

Once I had the fire going I turned to the business of seasoning the steaks but noticed the salt was missing. Celia was pouring the canister of Morton into the pitcher of water. I said nothing, just watched as the stream of salt thinned, the water clouding beneath it.

Celia lobbed the empty canister into the trashcan. Then she poured a glass, stirred with her finger, and chugged it in a single swallow. Afterwards, she gagged, her cheeks expanding, before she swallowed again.

"Now the steaks will be under-seasoned," I said. Then, "Are you all right?"

Her face sharpened into a cruel smile. She poured another glass and knocked it back with barroom bravado.

✳

When I went to bed that night Celia was asleep. I eased onto the mattress and scooted toward the warmth of her body. I closed my eyes and placed my hand on her stomach. It was small as a coconut, a knot with sloshing liquid inside. I let my fingers stretch over the skin, pressing firmly but carefully. I could feel the faint buzzing of our daughter's fins, her fluttering body suspended inside. And Celia, too. I could feel her heart pumping, pushing fluid, every beat the crest of a tiny wave. I could feel, as I lay there awake and alone, the strangeness of it all. Her swollen stomach, the fish swimming around inside of her — these facts seemed too wonderful and perilous to ever be true.

✳

Her thirst for salt aside, Celia was inscrutable as ever. She complained about her work at the studio even as she gracefully served our customers. She washed pickles down with glasses of milk. She watched recorded soap operas and commented on the lighting in every shot. *Where did this light designer study? The Funeral Home? Did that actor have plastic surgery or has he been embalmed?*

I'd started researching aquariums. I read online

reviews from fish owners around the globe. Most people, it seemed, felt only outrage about the containers to which they'd entrusted their fish. There were horror stories of tanks with poor centers of gravity, tanks tipping over in the night; tanks built of substandard glass by underpaid and undertrained children in the far reaches of the world. Cracks streaking through their walls, water seeping from their sides. People waking to find carcasses at the bottom of dry cases, air thick with briny decay.

One evening, when we were about to close up the portrait studio, I told Celia about one of the tragic Amazon reviews I'd read earlier that day. "This woman in Hong Kong, she lost a whole school of tigerfish."

Celia was on the computer, editing photos we'd shot that morning. Another suburban family.

"I think we should build our aquarium," I said.

She was zoomed in tight on a photo, the baby's head slackened onto its mother's bosom, its mouth open. "Have you ever noticed that babies are shaped like spider egg sacs?"

She was onto something. Viewed so closely, the baby had that unsettling, grotesque quality of nature in progress — something an unruly child might prod with a stick.

"If we build the tank we'll know it's made well," I said.

"What about the tank at my parents' house?" Celia asked.

"That thing belongs in a middle school classroom —

low-grade glass, questionable structural integrity, a tacky background."

She returned her attention to the computer screen; she began airbrushing the father's razor burn. "I'm not sure we can afford to build one," she said. "It would probably cost as much as our house."

"We'd actually save a lot building it ourselves," I said.

"Do you want to spend the rest of your life in this studio?" she asked.

"We're going to be parents," I said.

Celia's mouth pulled sideways, her left cheek dimpling — it was a face she often made. Back then I interpreted the expression as annoyance, but now I believe it was something closer to pity.

❈

There were moments, of course, when our feelings surfaced before darting away. Like the day we learned our daughter's species and, as a kind of celebration, went to the zoo. It was miserable weather for zoo-going, the air bristly with cold drizzle. I bought an umbrella emblazoned with the image of an elephant, the handle shaped like a trunk.

We had the place to ourselves, the sidewalks empty as we strolled past polar bears and sea lions, jaguars and apes. At the end of a cave-like hallway flush with the scent of fish, we entered a viewing room. There we stood in the dank shadows below an enormous window, a soft light shining down from the surface of the water, daylight refracted into scattered rays. Most of the fish were big listless bodies hanging in the cloudy tank. Every so often a school of small fish swirled past in a kaleidoscopic bloom.

"There's supposed to be a Spanish mackerel in here," I said.

"It might be hard to tell," Celia said. "They're sort of plain-looking."

A woman entered the viewing room, stopping at the edge of the tank. I continued to search for a mackerel as the woman slowly worked her way toward us. When she was standing next to me she whispered, "Look at all the fishies swimming around."

"Yes," I said, "Aren't they something?" But then I saw the little boy, a toddler, standing at her legs, his arms extended up to her hands. He had an unnatural, cleaned-up look, like the kids who came into the studio for portraits.

The woman smiled at me, then pulled him past us to the other end of the tank.

"You keep looking for the fish," Celia said. "I'm going to the concession stand."

"You don't want to see it?" I asked.

"We've seen the pictures already," she said.

"I thought you'd be more excited," I said.

"I'm exhausted," she said. "And to be honest, I'm a little tired of fish — we've talked about them all day."

"I'm trying to prepare," I said.

"You're excited to get a pet," she said.

We were silent, facing the aquarium, the truth of her words trickling into us. Before us the water quivered with the quiet gestures of all those fins.

❄

I moved forward on our aquarium, measuring the nursery, taping dimension markers to the floor. The tank would take up most of the room, with just enough space left over for us to maneuver, sit, observe. I ordered the finest materials — reinforced steel, tempered fiberglass, a zoo-quality aerator and drainage system — and we made arrangements for a team of contractors to install the plumbing.

I handled more and more of the work at the studio, to ensure that Celia got plenty of rest. During slow hours I'd thumb through the textbooks Celia's biologist loaned us. The world's waters were full of dangers, it seemed. There were the obvious threats — fishermen and predators and oil spills — but there were quiet killers too: diseases and poisonous plants and chemical exposure.

After reading a few pages I'd feel an ignorance so acute that it blurred my vision, the words clumping into a monolithic bulk, aloof as a mountaintop against the horizon. My gaze would lift from the textbook and settle on the over-lit aisles of PriceNipper, and I'd end up thinking about those months after I first met Celia. How I'd carried around a heaviness of feeling not unlike the exhilaration before taking a photograph. How we'd lived in that feeling, Celia and I, piecing our lives together inside of it like we were constructing a set. Like we were holding different poses. And for so many months — so many years — I'd braced myself, afraid of the clack of the lens, afraid of the dissipation that follows.

How long had it been since I'd felt that heady mixture of excitement and fear? How long had it been since I'd had something I was afraid to lose? During those slow days, alone at the studio, I tried to identify the precise moment when faked apathy became real boredom. Maybe during one of our infrequent arguments, when we'd hurled pent-up feelings at one another, words like fists, our voices violent. Or maybe after we'd talked ourselves out of selling the portrait studio, after we'd postponed Celia's idea to take our savings and find work in another city.

Or more likely it was a quiet event that passed quickly — one of those moments of obscure significance that dangles knifelike in memory. Perhaps it was that night, just after we'd closed up the studio, when I was cleaning my camera. As my eye settled over the viewfinder, a single breast came into focus. Resting in the 'V' of Celia's sweater, the breast stared at me with a bearing that could only be described as puckish, the nippled equivalent of a shit-eating grin. I instinctively snapped a photo.

Sometimes, as I'm sorting through my personal shots, I come across that image. It seems straightforward enough — Celia's delighted expression, her pleasure in disrupting the wholesome studio — but sometimes the camera reduces rather than apprehends; sometimes a photograph warms mystery until it looks like nostalgia. When I'd taken that photo of Celia, the room was trembling with a disgruntled energy the camera didn't capture.

✻

I woke up at sunrise one Saturday and went to the nursery, determined to construct the aquarium. My supplies were stacked neatly in the center of the room, my tool belt draped over them. I was arranging the base, placing the beams over the markers, when I sensed something above me. The mobile — it hung in the middle of the room, painted birds wincing in sleepy light. The arrangement of its pieces suggested an obscure order. Like the skeleton of some long-dead creature, pieced back together — the small-boned obsession of a minor archaeologist.

I decided to work around it, beneath it, until Celia and I could discuss its placement. All morning my hands fumbled over tools, scattering parts. But before long I settled into a rhythm, my grip steadying, the wrench turning truer.

I'd been working on the aquarium for a few hours when I glanced over to find Celia standing in the doorway.

"You're up earlier than I expected," I said.

"And you're further along than I expected," she said.

For a long moment we stared at each other in silence.

"You don't have to stop," she said.

I finished tightening a bolt.

"You like my addition?" she asked.

"It's an interesting mobile," I said, "but it'll be a bit

crowded in here."

"It's bigger than I expected," she said.

"How'd you hang it?" I asked.

She smiled — not her usual wry semi-smile, but the full spread, a whole octave of piano keys. That smile cut into my chest, my body recognizing how long it had been since she'd looked that happy. The mobile seemed to be communicating something neither of us could say.

She headed down the hall without a word and I continued to work. I was securing the last wall, closing myself into the fiberglass rectangle, when she returned with a handful of paint swatches. She flipped through them, stopping every once in a while to get my opinion.

"I like this one," she said, pressing a blue color against the fiberglass.

"I like it, too," I said. "What's it called?"

"Atlantic Blue."

❊

It happened before we were ready. I'd gone inside the grocery store to get Celia some yogurt while she waited in the car. When I came back, she was reclining. I climbed in quietly to avoid disturbing her. I had already started the engine when she said, "My saltwater just broke."

She said it calmly, the punchline to a joke she'd waited months to deliver.

"Do you feel her flopping?" I asked.

She rolled down her window, the car thick with brine.

"Is there any water left in there?"

She told me to shut up, to get us to the hospital. So that's what I did; it was only a couple of miles away. I sped along the interstate, my eyes darting from mirror to mirror as I changed lanes and zoomed through the traffic. Celia lay there in the seat, her hand on her forehead, breathing in time with the soft music of the radio, a pleading fifties song.

Ten minutes later we were rushed to the maternity floor, where Celia settled into a birthing pool and delivered a fish the size of a rolled-up Sunday newspaper — two pounds, three ounces. They gave us a private room, placing our daughter in a tank beside Celia's bed. Lying there in her hospital gown, Celia looked like she'd been lost at sea, her skin all wrinkled from the prolonged submersion, her hair damp and curly.

Our daughter's scales had a bluish hue, yellow dots along the side, slender fins waving in the water.

"I was worried she might have bulging eyeballs," Celia said. "But they haven't grown since the ultrasound."

"I think she has my lips," I said. "Not as full as yours."

"Her name is Lily," Celia said. "I always wanted a Lily."

The next morning, after her birth certificate had been marked with her tailfin print, we strapped Lily's portable aquarium into the car. It was supposed to be splash-proof, but I drove home with my foot kissing the brake pedal, the water sloshing with every turn we made.

❄

Lily waited patiently in her portable tank while we
finished preparing the nursery. We spent the morning
installing red mangroves, filling the aquarium with
saltwater, and stocking a variety of smaller fish. Once
everything was ready, we prepared to transition Lily to
her new home.

I was about to reach into the portable tank when
Celia stopped me.

"You forgot to put these on," she said, passing me
the gloves we'd purchased — they were designed to
prevent the oils of our palms from harming her scales.

The rubber chirped as I pulled the gloves tight.
When I reached inside the tank, Lily darted from my
fingers.

"She's terrified," I said.

"I would be too," Celia said.

I cupped my hand under her belly, gripped behind
the pectoral fins. Then I lifted her from the bowl and
lowered her over the chest-high wall of the aquarium.
She was still for a moment but then, with a flip of her
tail, splashed down into the water. She stopped by the
aerator, bubbles fluttering around her.

"Should we get the camera?" I asked.

"Not right now," Celia said. "Let's just watch."

We sat on the floor, leaned our backs against the
wall. We watched in silence as she mingled with other
fish, as she ate her first sand perch, as she flashed
around the tank, absorbed by the world we'd created for
her.

"It's missing something," Celia said.

"We followed all the installation instructions," I said.

"The tank just looks naked. Sort of institutional."

"The décor is a bit modern," I said.

A minute later, my eyes drifted up to the mobile. It was hanging there above us, insistent as an idea, fully formed, waiting to be acknowledged.

I used the step stool to unhook it from the ceiling and then I latched it to the cross beam at the top of the aquarium. I dropped the mobile into the water, letting its pieces sink into place.

"What do you think?" I asked.

"I'm not sure Aunt Lucille would approve," she said. "But Lily seems to love it."

Lily flitted around and between the mobile, the tin birds dancing in her current.

❋

We spent that first day moving distractedly about the house. For a while Celia carried the baby monitor, listening to the sound of the aquarium, but she turned it off to watch her recorded soap operas. I kept finding myself back in the nursery, checking the water level, the temperature, the salinity. I wanted to have something to *do*, but already one thing seemed clear: it would be painfully easy to raise a fish.

Late in the afternoon, I decided to move a loveseat from our office into the nursery. Celia and I brought our cameras into the room, but instead of taking pictures we sat there drinking coffee beside Lily, who lingered in the corner closest to us. With the aerator mumbling hypnotically, I experienced a softening of my consciousness. The room wobbling with late afternoon light, air thick as liquid — it seemed like Lily, Celia, and I were sharing a container, our house its own kind of tank. And I could feel, beyond our house, a whole planet stacked with habitats, a big world made of little worlds. The three of us suspended there in our small compartment of time and space, hoping in some unconscious way that all of it — everything — would hold together for a few moments longer. That the pressurized walls of the aquarium would withstand... That water would keep pumping through the city's rusted pipes. That gravity would continue to steady our poses.

As afternoon shaded into evening, the sun dragged its light from the room. The salty air had expanded my lungs, filling them with heavy oxygen. I was beginning to feel sleepy.

That's when Celia asked, "What are those little red fish?"

At first I didn't understand, but then I noticed a spark of red toward the back of the aquarium. I looked closer and saw other colors, too — yellow and blue, orange and green. I approached the tank, turned on its floor light.

A liquid galaxy appeared, a constellation of paint flakes surrounding the mobile's pieces, silver clouding over the light. Lily hung in the middle, moonlike.

For a moment, we couldn't understand what we were seeing. We didn't recognize the slivers of paint.

And we couldn't anticipate the chemical exposure, the long weeks of testing and treatment, the biologist's endless visits.

In that moment, what Celia and I shared was not panic but something like wonder.

I raised my camera and stilled my eye behind it.

Weight

It's your birthday. You sit in your room finishing homework and listening to music while you wait for him. The Disney channel is on but the volume is down. Your room is small, and all your furniture is made of wicker. You're beginning to feel like you're sleeping in the dollhouse tucked away in your closet. Your mom wants you to donate the dollhouse, tells you about all the extra closet space you could have, but you can't bring yourself to do it.

Headlights flash onto your bedroom wall. You look out the window but it's not who you are hoping for. It's your dad. He wears a St. Louis Cardinals visor and an old Mark McGwire jersey. Every year since you were a baby he has taken your family on the same vacation, a week in St. Louis. It's the kind of vacation people go on so they can say they went on vacation. You spend half the trip inside Busch stadium eating eight dollar ice cream that melts before you finish it, clapping when everyone else does. You spend the other half staring at boys, determining which ones are afraid of you and which ones aren't. You're starting to understand that you're beautiful, that people aren't just saying that because it's what you want to hear. You've noticed your mom doesn't say it anymore.

Your dad knocks on your door before he opens it. He smells like cedar, and he wears a cell phone in a holster

on his hip. You normally make fun of him for everything he does, but you've stopped for now, while he's
living at the motel down the street. As soon as he gets
an apartment he will be fair game again.

He looks at you and shakes his head. "Sixteen?" he
says, but it's not really a question. He's not that kind of
father.

He leans halfway over for an awkward hug, the kind
he might give to a coworker or a church friend. Then he
pulls out his wallet and hands you two hundred dollar
bills. It is more than he's ever given you, the most
anyone has ever given you, but you don't say anything
about that. You thank him and reach around him for a
real hug, the kind he's forgotten how to give. He talks
about insurance for a while and then he leaves. When
he's gone you put one of the bills in your wallet and you
lay the other flat inside the pages of the Bible on your
wicker bedside table.

Another pair of headlights flashes into the driveway.
You're certain who it is this time. You stand up on your
bed to look at yourself in the mirror, combing your
hands through your long brown hair. You're convinced
that your body fluctuates daily, that some days your
boobs are big and your legs small, that some days it's
the other way around. But today is not one of those
days. Today is your birthday. Your legs seem tiny,
barely big enough to hold you up, and your boobs feel
swollen. On days like today your boobs make you feel
bulletproof, like the knots of flesh on your chest could

protect you from anything, like your heart is safe behind them.

The doorbell rings. You run to answer it because you don't want your mom to. She's in the living room watching America's Funniest Home Videos. She laughs at all the clips, especially the ones with pets in them. She is obsessed with reality television. Since your father moved out she's started calling herself "The Bachelorette."

When you open the door, he's holding a single red rose. His hair is shaggy, his bangs in his eyes, and he's wearing a shirt without sleeves. He hasn't cut them off; he bought the shirt that way. He smells like a dressing room at the mall, like cologne and cigarettes. He kisses you in the doorway, a soggy, scouring kiss. It is still light outside. You wonder if your neighbors can see you. The thought of that embarrasses and excites you at the same time. While he's kissing you, you rub your fingers along the muscled lump of his bicep. Your sexuality is hyper but malleable, still shaped more by rumor and expectation than by anything you actually feel. The girls you sit with during lunch have decided arms are important, arms are sexy, and so now you pay particular attention to his. It's an easy thing to do since his shirts almost never have sleeves.

You grab his hand and lead him inside. You take him to the kitchen, hoping your mom will stay in the living room. There's a cake on the kitchen counter. Your mom picked it up from the Wal-Mart deli. It says, HAPPY SWEET SIXTEEN NIKOLE!!! You can't believe they spelled your name correctly. The spelling of your name makes you proud. There are seven Nicoles in your class. You are the only Nikole. Someday you'll understand what it means that your name is spelled differently. Someday, when you're selling pharmaceuticals in a place that would now seem inconceivably big, inconceivably urbane, some place like Nashville or Atlanta or even Birmingham, you'll blush at the provincial spelling of your name. But not now. Now you're sixteen and you live in rural Arkansas and it's your birthday.

The cake is yellow with white icing. You tried a piece earlier but you didn't like it. It tasted like the smell of a magic marker, the kind you use to write tightly scripted notes to your boyfriend. In the notes you try to tell him how you feel about him, but it never seems like enough. The words, no matter how hard you press the marker against the page, fail to convey the intensity of your emotions. The rigid purple letters on your wide-ruled paper are the sickly cousins of the flares in your chest cavity, those searing feelings that burn your body down to gauze and let the whole universe pass through you.

So you don't like the cake. But he does. He's on his third piece already, eating it with his hands and talking with his mouth full. Your mom walks into the kitchen. She rolls her eyes when she sees him. Your mom is not a person. She is your mom, a servant who's no longer useful, who's starting to get in the way. You remember when you cared about her opinion. You remember when she was pretty, but time has pinched her face. Time has thinned her stringy black hair to transparency. Time has made her stupid.

She's bending over, leaning into the fridge, when she asks what y'all are up to. He shrugs and lowers his eyes. You completely ignore her. She pulls out a can of Miller Lite. She says it's Miller time. She seems to have an endless catalogue of drinking clichés. But you've never noticed. You don't pay attention to anything she says, and for the most part, you're not missing much. She pops the beer open and stares, looking back and forth between the two of you.

"How many calories does that have?" you ask.

"Not very many. I'm drinking my dinner. You and your calories, it's an unhealthy obsession."

"Drinking isn't healthy. It kills brain cells. Mrs. Milton said it causes memory loss."

"Charlotte Milton really shouldn't be teaching health class." She shakes her head and takes a long drink. "She wears a wig."

"What's that have to do with health class?" you ask. Your boyfriend never says anything in front of your mom. You wish he would speak. You wish he would do something to make her less suspicious. He could smile at least, but he doesn't. He just scratches his neck and stares at the floor, looking at the peeling brown linoleum like it's a piece of abstract art. In more ways than you'll ever know, it is. In more ways than you'll ever know, that peeling brown linoleum tells the whole story.

"I'm just saying, it doesn't make any sense to have a sick woman teaching health class."

✲

You're in his truck. You like that it's an extended cab, but you wish it had automatic locks and windows. You feel like you should be the one driving, but you're not. After all, it's your birthday. And not just any birthday, your *sixteenth* birthday. The radio is on a country station. He likes a brand of rock that's all screeches and reverb and oily bangs, and you like top forty music. Neither of you likes country music. You have that in common, and listening to it reminds you of that fact.

You know where you're going. You've been arranging it for a long time. You've been arranging it since he asked for a piece of gum in Mrs. Milton's class. You've been arranging it in breathy, late-night whispers over the telephone, ringlets of phone cord wrapped around your wrist. Every word, everything you have exchanged with him has been a negotiation of this night, of this event.

There's a weightlessness in his truck, a stillness. It's as though the nighttime — the burning rice fields and liquid air and brimming moon — is passing through the two of you, not the other way around. A single word might disrupt it, might bring all of it — the truck, the music, the night — to a screeching halt. And so you don't speak. The two of you get this part of the story right: neither of you utters a single fucking word. And before you know it, just as you'd settled into the anti-gravity silence, you're there.

It's a single-wide trailer in the middle of a flat empty field. It's not at all as you had imagined it. He had called it his hunting *club*. You'd pictured a cabin in the middle of the woods, someplace rustic and beautiful, smelling of the oak it was carved from. For most of your life you've been a fit-thrower, tyrannically intolerant of the disparities between your expectations and reality. But not tonight. Tonight is the night you swallow the world's offer of disappointment, consume it eagerly, even. And it's a good thing too, because there's plenty in store for you. That new car you've been begging for? You'll inherit your grandmother's '91 Lumina your senior year, after she hacks up the bloody last of her lungs. A good college? Try the local community college. Medical school someday, if you really, really bust your ass? C- in organic chemistry. Your parents' marriage? Please, *please* let's not get started on your fucking parents.

But none of that is tonight. None of that is now. Now he's telling you to wait as he opens his door. For a second you worry that he's going to leave you here in the dark, sitting alone in his truck, but then he's opening your door, helping you down. He's a gentleman, earnest in sleeveless chivalry. You grab his hand and he pulls you up the porch stairs propped in front of the trailer, the porch that had, many years ago, been someone's drunken foray into carpentry. You don't notice the swollen electric globe of the moon. You don't notice the sky yawning above you.

Inside, he flips a light switch and musty yellow leaks down from a bare bulb. You are surprised, but not bothered, by the number of dead animals hanging around the room. Antlered deer heads leer at you, their grotesque shadows cast black against grainy white walls. Bird bodies perch on crooked sticks, poised, it seems, for flight. In the kitchen, a turkey roosts on top of the refrigerator.

He opens the fridge door to reveal a baffling variety of cheap light beers, the cans stacked and prismatic, gleaming like bricks of polished silver. He pulls one out, pinches it open, and offers it. You take a drink, your face shriveling with the bitterness, and hand it back to him. The two of you stand there and pass the beer back and forth, taking constricted sips, until there's nothing left in the can, not even a drop, and it's like you're drinking the aluminum air.

❊

It may be your birthday but it's a weeknight. You don't have all night. You've got a curfew. Your mom will be waiting for you in the living room, comatose from distilled reality and Miller Light. You decide it's time to act. You take his hand and pull him down a narrow hallway, toward a dark room at its end.

It takes your eyes a moment to adjust to the darkness. Bunk beds are stacked around the room like cages at the animal shelter, their wooden frames skeletal, almost, in the light that lags through the doorway. You grab his arms just below the shoulder and pull him toward you. You kiss him. It's not like the kiss earlier, the one on your doorstep. There's a distance to this kiss, a withholding of something that you don't recognize.

He pulls your shirt off, over your head, and you tug at his, but it won't come off. You've never undressed anyone before. It's like wrestling with a mannequin in the dark. You finally give up. You back away and start pulling your own clothes off. You watch him do the same. This works much better — just pretend you're getting ready to climb into the bathtub.

He is on top of you now. Your head rests on a pillow that smells like syrupy pancakes. Your back clings to the cool nylon of a flimsy mattress. Your hands grip its tattered edges. He pushes his body closer to yours, his scrawny legs warming against your thighs. You've heard a lot of discussion about this. Your more experienced friends have told you a million different horror stories. None of them are true. Not now, at least.

As part of him presses, cuts, into you, you feel like the frog you dissected two weeks ago in biology class, its squishy carcass splayed on a stainless steel tray, lifeless beneath the blade of your scalpel. You know that what's happening is much bigger, much more important, than it seems. But you're not sure why. That's okay. That's normal. Welcome to a world where gravity is made of doubt.

❄

You get dressed in silence, but you talk in his truck. Both of you sing along to a Garth Brooks song. The ride home feels like you are returning from a long trip, feels like you're returning from vacation. You're surprised by how little things have changed while you were gone. And when you walk in the door of your house, when you find your mom waiting where you knew she would be, you are glad — glad to see her watching a show involving a hot tub full of screaming, shirtless people.

She asks if you've had a good birthday and you nod your head. She asks how much money your father gave you, and you lie. You tell her he gave you a hundred dollars, same as her. She shakes her head. You tell her you're going to bed, and then you do.

You close the door behind you. Your TV is still on from earlier, flashing the bright shadows of the Disney Channel on your walls. You check the pages of your Bible to make sure the hundred dollar bill is in there. You put on your pajamas, sprawl out on top of the covers, and turn the volume up. It's Hannah Montana, your favorite show. You watch for a few minutes, but you've seen this episode before. You turn the TV off. You lie there in the darkness, listening to the nighttime hum of your house, until you roll over onto your stomach, the way you normally sleep. You look up at your headboard. The white paint is starting to chip off of the wicker, naked brown strands checkering across its surface. You rub your hand over it. It feels grainy and brittle. It feels weak. The wicker all around you seems so fragile, but it keeps holding you up.

The Wavering Grass

I.

The other cows — Herefords and Limousines, mostly —
were obsessed with escape; they roamed the fence days
on end, hunting busted barbed wire. Not Muriel, the
Angus. Even then it was obvious she was the smartest
in the herd. She would stand in the sage grass at the
foot of a persimmon tree, her face pensive as she
mouthed fruits. Jaw rolling, tongue flicking seeds.
When air concussed overhead and tree limbs trembled
— a thunderstorm's signals — she always went to the
barn, even while the other cows scattered like lice in the
pasture's green fur: mouths open, licking skyward. And
she'd always be the last to show when Albert arrived
with paint brush and tick chemicals. Or when he penned
them up, one by one, and lit into them with hormone-
cocked syringes.

She'd recognized, even as a yearling, that escape was
just a different kind of ruin. That fugitives were napped
into a stranger's trailer, delivered to the sale barn — a
hot, dusty wait for the butcher's blade. Or even worse
— turned up car-smacked, snap-ribbed, a buzzard
buffet. Muriel didn't waste her time at the trampled
property line. She had a steady supply of grass, and that
was plenty.

It always had been, actually. Even in the hanging
cradle of her mother's belly, she'd grown by a grass fat
mainline. Pressure, breath, hunger — these were her

first sensations. Until it was time to come into sun, those choked hours of muscle strain and pain. And then, from outside — smooth hands clamping her legs, pulling her into harsh, hard light. Hours spent in warm grass wetted by her blood-slick body. Her mother's licks, heavy and coarse, blind strokes of animal love. Muriel still feeling, as she lay in the sun, the grip of the hands that had pulled her into the world.

Her legs, wobbly at first, stoutened and stiffened. Years waved through the hot grass, trickled through melting snow. She grew taller, fatter. Time charted across the visits of Albert — that upright god whose hands now dispensed pain: needle-prick serums and metal-taste minerals and hide-blistering compounds.

She'd withdraw into the grass. The very grass where she lay during that first afternoon. Oh, the grass! How could a body want and want so? She passed days plucking tufts, blades dangling from her jaws. Grass tearing up, channeling to her stomach, clumping around her hindquarters.

And there, in the thick of her backside, grew another wanting. The ache to get bigger, fatter still. Hard-kerneled longing in the meat of her, like seeds in a persimmon middle. She stood horny for a whole summer. The sky wavering above, a blue monolith, tinted and trembling. What to do but stand beneath the sky? Land heat-cooked under her hooves. Hindquarters stacked around ancient desire, a buried vault, undiscovered. Waiting.

She spent restless days in the shade of a leaning barn. Waiting, waiting. And one morning it happened — a trailer delivered the bull, a Brahmin, pent up and ornery. She watched as a man in faded army fatigues, a man who wasn't Albert, opened the trailer door. The bull's hooves clapped the trailer floor, his haunches rattling the walls. Albert and the army man wrangled the bull into the corral, where she was waiting. She didn't protest like the other heifers, those filibustering rituals; no, she trotted to the ring's center and stood, queenly and expectant — submission untainted by the indignity of evasion.

The men stood by as the bull circled her, heavy breaths and hoof scratching. She waited there in the rising dust of his commotion, dirt specks wafting onto her, the long summer's heat beaten into her sweaty hide. Her hips cracked open, spine softening, ready for the bull, ready to collapse into his heavy violence, his hulking fuck.

And finally he arrived, pushing onto her. She stared into the grass, insects shivering between stalks. The sun lay alkaline overhead, its own hot violence, its churning middle, ironing down the landscape. As the Brahmin torqued, she saw, at her periphery, Albert's stolid face, his hat held at his hip, his quiet observance of the moment.

Muriel realized then what the other cows would never know: that cattle were his one luxury. She sensed the hours he spent fixing mechanical watches, his hands cramping as he wheedled those tiny insides, parts twitching like little beetles. She could feel, in his past, those gaunt days of weighing his money against the price of meat — discounted chicken or remaindered beef? She knew he'd pieced together watch after watch, hands blue with arthritis, hoping that one day he'd need consider just one simple question: sell or slaughter?

✳

II.

After the bull, months spent under changing sky, summer's hardness softening to autumn. Her insides softened too. The bull had enlivened her body, made it delicate, even as her bones thickened. She was nosing grass one afternoon, sore-jawed and hungry, when she saw a bloody tooth lying in clumped alfalfa. Other teeth followed, her skull spitting them out. Milk teeth, bloody bits of bone, scattered in scalded grass.

And the growing that followed the bull's visit: ribs widening, belly distending. Everything bloated. Even her organs swelling. A tom-tom heart, punching blood through her body; her uterus thickening, amniotic matter gelling into muscle and bone. Muscle and bone clotting into a cow-shaped mass. Was this to be expected? Was any of this to be expected? The wavering grass, the upturned ocean of the sky, the four-legged train car that was her body — were these to be expected?

Her body grew obscene for its size, an absurd tumescence. Her belly didn't lower but widened, her ribs bending around the calf, a cradle of bone. The kicks —

jabs lancing her insides, like she'd swallowed something lively, something vile. And months later, contractions. Heaving and pushing. Deep, wheezing breaths.

And still no calf. All the flexing, straining, breathing, but no calf: only a leg dangling from her backside. A body wrenched, racked. She needed to be alone with her throbbing misery. She carried herself away from the barn and past the feed troughs and past the ponds, to the lowest ground, a dry creek bed.

It was a kind of dry heaving, her body retching without release. The bull had opened her up, but not enough for what was here — a Brahmin-bred calf in an Angus. It wasn't sensible. But there had been nothing sensible in her longing, her need for the bull.

An oversized calf plugged in her middle. The problem a matter of direction; the problem an ass-first exit. She lay down. The ground pushing against her belly, easing the pain, somehow. Panting in the grass, she felt a disorientation like she'd had the afternoon she was born, the world turned inside out.

The sky tall now, the sun sunken beyond the horizon's leafy dam. In the distance she heard feed pans clanging — Albert, come to count the herd. To call them to the barn. To check on the bull-heavied heifers. She crawled deeper into the grass, her belly dragging the ground as she pushed. As though the pressure might turn the calf around.

In the low gloom hung an evening moon, fat as an apple, sudden as the hot head of the branding iron. Then Albert appeared at the edge of the brush, calling *Heyo,*

Heyo. He stepped closer, sensing her presence. She studied him, the grass stalks splintering her vision. The worn lines of his suit, the oil-parted hair, the arthritic hands, knuckles like lug nuts. His skin softly pigmented, a bruised fruit. Still, he'd kept the same ready posture, the same hungry lean.

He stepped closer, eyes locked on her. Muriel watched his hands. His hands that had pulled her into the world of grass, below the big sky. Now, with the calf aching inside her like a giant rotten tooth, she needed his hands. This needing the worst since the bull's visit.

Albert circled her slowly, eyes pressing on her hide. He produced a pair of rubber gloves, stretched them over his fingers. Then he stepped behind her and began pulling the calf. This sensation oddly similar to that first pain inflicted by the bull — it hurt, yes, but with satisfying purpose. A tension to be released through its own aggravation. She opened herself to it, legs spreading, spine slackening. The calf's progress slow but fully felt, Albert's strong hands relieving her wearied muscles.

But then a searing pang ripped through her hindquarters. The throbbing loosed itself from her midsection, saturated the rest of her. Her legs stiffened, body lifting from the ground. Agony seized her, its clutch euphoric. She was giddy with hurt, the pain its own splendid dimension — she was standing inside of it.

Albert cursed. His voice slitted through the formless

noise of the pain, and her body absorbed his words —
within those sounds she felt old knowledge, gentle
sensations, memory's delirium. There was Albert as a
little boy, seated at a roughshod table. Outside the
window, snowflakes blinking down, thick as biscuit
flour. The sallow skin of a younger brother, cries
hissing sickly from a cornered crib. This was the day
his mother handed him the cleaver, told him to slaughter the pig — the last of their winter meat — and carry
it across the pasture to the neighbors they owed.

It was then, as she remembered that old knife, that
Muriel sensed the cool metal melting through her
groin. She'd seen this knife before — applied to feed
bags, to hay bale twine. Now the blade edged through
her belly, her belly spilling open, the calf hanging there.
As the knife worked, Muriel thought about that day
when Albert had handled the pig. How he dragged the
animal through the snow, blood gurgling from the slit
throat, burps of steam rising. How he left the pig with a
flank-armed farm woman. How he followed the blood
trail back across the pasture until new snow blotted it
out.

Now Muriel was death standing, Albert grappling
with the half-born calf. Her shock surged into a
muscled fit, spinning and bucking. Her skull smashed
against his chest, flipping him onto his back. Her
hooves stamped Albert's torso. Ribs slivered his heart.

Albert lay there, his hands outstretched and still.
Muriel settled beside him, the two of them crowding
death in the pickled light of dusk.

She spent these last minutes in another memory, the time Albert left home. Abandoned the tree-rotten hills of Arkansas — that starving farmland — to head for the Boeing factory in Seattle. The job, the city, the new life — these things would ruin quickly. But Muriel rested inside that earlier moment, on the way to Seattle. She listened to the steel gallop of train wheels, Albert's body jostling westward. He was seventeen years old and sipping seltzer beside the broad window of the dining car. Outside, the plains dragging backwards beneath a marble-slab sky — a whole sprawled continent of grass, dense and green and delicious, bristling under the sun.

The Pond Robber

After his father died, and after his mother was shepherded
over to Nurturing Hills Nursing Estate, Murray
Thornwiler relocated to the old family homestead to
become custodian of the pasture. The pond there was
the lifelong project of his father, Horace, who had
imported a rare strain of Japanese catfish — rumored to
be the only such stock in all the waters of Arkansas. To
protect these peerless creatures Horace had allowed
fishing solely on days he deemed worthy of the sport.
Every Thanksgiving, for instance, the Thornwilers
would pack up leftovers and drive out to the levee,
where they baited hooks with scraps of turkey fat. On
their birthdays the Thornwiler children would wake to
find gift-wrapped cans of Spam, their father's bait of
choice. At Christmas, when most families gathered
around scrubby cedar trees, the Thornwilers collected
at the pond, three acres of liquid citrine jeweled
between sloping hillsides. Their hands shivered around
fishing poles, until they ran out of the homemade blood-
bait Murray's mother baked during the holidays.

Murray had been settled on the family property only
a few months when the pond disturbances began. The
trouble started on the eastern edge of the county. Cattle
farmers rode out to check their herds and discovered
dead fish lining the banks of watering holes, stone-eyed
carcasses washed into hoof prints. News of the ravaged

waters swept through the countryside, one farm to another, swift as the rotten wind that accompanied the deaths. At first the authorities believed the die-offs were the result of a plague: bacteria leaching through springs, passing pond to pond. But when Izard County officials tested the lifeless waters and found trace elements of nitroglycerin, they determined there was a fish-bomber at large. A pond robber, as county residents described the culprit.

Some pond owners held candlelit vigils late into the night, guarding against explosive notions. Others focused on pursuing the criminal; Robert Niffler, for example, delivered three head of bermuda-fat cattle to the county courthouse — a bovine bounty. A few people resorted to more fatalistic measures. Jerry Thurnstile sunk ten sticks of dynamite into his own perfectly good pond, this reported by the *Izard County Register*, because he couldn't tolerate the thought of someone else wrecking his property.

As most county residents panicked, Murray tried to avoid the uproar. He noticed that the victims typically occupied those shabbier corners of the county where lazy landowners let fences lapse, where ponds were glorified puddles. So Murray decided to concentrate on tasks that better suited him. Cooking Cornish game hens, for instance. They were very difficult to marinate — too much worcestershire and they were salty; too little, a gamy flavor. Delicate negotiations like this were, unfortunately, interrupted from time to time, such as on the afternoon when, nearing a perfect marinade, he looked out the kitchen window and saw a horse grazing in his backyard.

It was a tall appaloosa, its dark brown coat marbled with white. He stepped out to the patio and looked around. No one, nothing but the horse. It was bridled and saddled, bulging bags hanging over its ribs. It had been ridden a good distance — coat slick with sweat, mane frizzy. He walked across the lawn and leaned beside the horse's belly — a mare, apparently. He petted her neck, ruffled her mane. The animal pressed into his hand, forcefully accepting his attention.

"I don't have any apples," he said.

The horse raised its head, continued chewing grass.

"A country gentleman ought to keep apples on hand," he said.

The horse bent down, plucked another bite of Murray's lawn.

"What does one do with a horse?" Murray asked the horse.

He needed to go back inside, give Irene a call. This was her sort of territory — her sister had horses, didn't she? Perhaps it was an aunt. Someone had horses.

Irene, it must be understood, was Murray's live-in assistant and his lone noteworthy companion after his two sons — products of separate failed marriages — moved away to operate dental practices in distant cities. She all but ran the Chevrolet dealership Murray had inherited and, once she turned sixty-five, began volunteering as a page at the senior citizens' library. And with a dynamite-toting lunatic roaming the county, she now had another task to manage.

When Murray returned to the kitchen he was surprised to find his brother Cecil seated at the table. Cecil was in some kind of Indian costume — feathers and tassels, buckskin and beads. His hair, though transparent at the scalp, draped to his shoulders, flattened against his temples by a headband. The getup seemed to belong on one of the Saturday morning Westerns the two of them had watched together as kids.

His brother hadn't been around in a handful of years — since their father's funeral, when Cecil had shown up wearing a sort of biker tuxedo, a startling combination of leather and denim. As a matter of decency Murray avoided commenting on such personal modifications — stylistic departures or haircuts or tattoos — because he found these changes so personal as to be obscene. But this Indian garb tested his resolve.

"I can't believe you're here," Cecil said.

"I live here," Murray said, sitting down across from him.

"I see you've done some remodeling," Cecil said.

Murray nodded. "Took out the old fridge. Replaced the cabinets. Pulled up the linoleum and put down tile."

"Has Mom seen it?"

"She refuses to leave the living center. I call her every once in a while, try to get her out, but she says she's done everything she wants to do."

"That's not what she tells me," Cecil said.

"What's she tell you?"

"That you never call."

Cecil had always taken peculiar pride in his neediness, in the fact that, despite his many personal troubles, he dutifully kept in touch with their mother. Murray pointed toward the backyard. "Where'd the horse come from?"

"I bought Alice a few months ago. Keep her at Lynwood Jackson's place. I come over to ride her from time to time."

"You drive from Memphis to ride a horse?" Murray asked.

Cecil belched loudly, the robust emission answering — positively — Murray's question. Murray thought momentarily of the dog they'd shared as kids, how Cecil had always come up with excuses for avoiding the less pleasant aspects of pet ownership.

"You been out to the pond lately?" Cecil asked.

"Irene's taking care of it," Murray said.

"I've been keeping up with the pond robber stuff online," Cecil said.

"Irene's very responsible," Murray said. Which reminded him — wasn't she supposed to pick up some Greek seasoning? Another instruction to give her. Sometimes Murray thought he might need to employ someone to keep Irene on task — a professional reminder.

"She your new pinch?" Cecil asked.

"If that's Memphis parlance for paramour, the answer is no," Murray said. "She's my personal assistant."

Cecil looked out the kitchen window. The horse was nosing the green shrubs that bordered the back of the house. "Those aren't pokeweed bushes are they? I can't have her eating those again."

Murray followed his brother outside. Cecil summoned the horse by pulling a carton of candy from his pocket and rattling the pieces like a maraca. The horse hurried over and Cecil tipped one of the candies into his hand. He extended his arm, palm up.

"What is that?" Murray asked.

"Gobstopper," Cecil said.

The horse's lips slurped as she sucked on the candy. Cecil climbed onto her back and sat there, squinting into the afternoon sun.

"What're you doing?" Murray asked.

"Waiting on you," Cecil said.

"To do what?"

Cecil leaned out, over the horse's ribs, and spit into Murray's yard. "I thought we'd go out and check on the pond."

"You're going to take the horse?"

"I don't get to ride her as often as I want," Cecil said. "Are you going to get on or not?"

Murray hadn't been on a horse since childhood. "Aren't we too big to ride double?"

"I specifically requested a model I could ride double on. Jackson said this was the one."

"I'm not getting on that horse," Murray said.

Then he approached the horse, slipped his foot into the stirrup, and lifted himself onto her back. He gripped the saddle and Cecil clicked his tongue, the noise setting the animal in motion.

They'd traveled a couple hundred yards when Cecil asked, "Would you give her a kick for me? You're blocking her ribs."

Murray scraped at the horse's midsection with the toe of his sneaker.

"I didn't ask you to scratch her," Cecil said. "Horses crave discipline." He reached around Murray to spank Alice, but she didn't move any faster. Their bodies rocked back and forth in rhythm with the horse's steps, the saddle creaking under their weight.

"Sometimes she gets sluggish after a snack," Cecil said.

Murray was wondering if they'd reach the pond before dark.

"Sugar crash, I think," said Cecil.

Halfway to the pond, Cecil reached into the tooled leather saddlebag and pulled out a prescription bottle. He popped the lid off and held the bottle to his mouth, tipping it back carefully, like a cattleman tilting his canteen during a dry spell. He leaned his head back and mumbled, "Back's giving me a lot of trouble."

"Could be these new equestrian tendencies of yours," Murray said. His ass was starting to hurt — a horse spine was anything but a proper seat.

Cecil leaned forward, then back again. "I don't think

so. Doctor told me all the jangling around would be good for my spinal column."

Alice paid little attention to Cecil's guidance of the reins, abandoning the road they traveled. "You've done such a poor job maintaining the road that she doesn't know she's off of it."

"My bushhogger has liver problems. He's been in the hospital for a month."

"I bet the pond robber's already come and gone. Who'd have noticed?"

Murray tried to ignore these little barbs. After all, Cecil had abandoned family obligations when he moved to Memphis and opened a golf cart dealership.

By the time they reached the pond, the sun leaned on the horizon, light weeping over the treeline. Cecil directed Alice to the pond's edge, where she bent her neck and lapped at the mud-clouded water. Murray and Cecil remained on her back.

They giggled at the slurping noise.

"The water's so thick with sludge," Cecil said, "I'm afraid she'll have to chew it."

The water's surface held the calm and color of the twilight. The pond's purpose had always been more spiritual than sporting. During its fifty-year history only four fish had ever been kept — the first fish landed by each of the Thornwiler children. All four were taken to a catfish taxidermist in Little Rock, where they were mounted and fitted with a plaque noting their weight and measurements. These trophies had hung in the Thornwiler living room as surrogates to the photos displayed by most families. Cecil's fish had been of respectable size — a four-pounder — but it was a curiously ugly specimen. Its head was misshapen, its skin jaundiced — and this unhealthy sheen worsened when the taxidermist tried to improve it. Murray's fish, on the other hand, was of a regal sort. Eight pounds, six ounces, and pretty as a vine-ripe tomato. It had hung over the mantel, the centerpiece of the room, coveted by half the county. The Cadillac of catfish, their father had called it.

Cecil reached around Murray's legs into his saddle-bag and pulled out a styrofoam carton. He peeled off the lid to reveal a slimy pink meat. Chicken livers, Murray guessed.

"Is there anything you don't have in those fucking saddlebags?" Murray asked.

"You want to do the honors?" Cecil asked, holding out the carton.

Murray grabbed a plug of raw liver and without ceremony tossed it into the water. The two of them waited, eyeing the meat as grease clouded around it. Though Cecil was seated in front of him, Murray thought he detected in his brother's posture the hope that the fish were already dead. Alice lifted her head, muzzle dripping, and looked forward as though she too were watching the water. Then a catfish, fat as a football, nodded up and sucked the liver down.

❈

When they arrived back at the house, Cecil tied up Alice in the carport next to Irene's car. Murray watched Cecil undress the horse. "Don't you think this concrete will hurt her feet?"

"She doesn't have feet," Cecil said.

"Okay, it'll hurt her hooves," Murray said.

"Her shoes are made of steel," Cecil said.

Murray untied the horse and led her into the front yard where he tied her to a leafless persimmon tree. Cecil scowled, a teenager's haughty expression of displeasure.

Inside, they found Irene sitting on the living room couch watching the real estate channel: photos of houses and sketches of floor plans, backed by squawking saxophone music — it sounded like the musician had a head cold.

After properly introducing Cecil to Irene, Murray took a seat beside her on the couch. Meanwhile Cecil wandered around the room, his breath whistling disapproval of Murray's décor adjustments.

"Murray, where are our fish?"

"They're in your old room," Murray said. "It's my office now."

"You've converted my bedroom to an office?" Cecil asked. "Where am I to sleep?"

"You could sleep in Cindy's old room," Murray said. And then he asked, "You're staying here?"

"I thought we'd get this guy together."

"What guy?"

"The pond robber, Murray," Cecil said. He smiled at Irene as though Murray's dimwittedness was difficult to fathom. "I intend to relocate to the pond bank tomorrow."

"He may not come for weeks," Murray said. "He may not come at all. Weren't you going to ask my permission?"

"I won't use more than my third of the property," Cecil said.

It took Murray a moment to figure out what Cecil meant. "Mom technically still owns the place."

"I've already talked to her about it. She doesn't mind if Alice and I stay here with you for a while."

"What about your dealership?"

"You know how it is, Murray. You sell golf carts. You don't sell golf carts."

Murray nodded, figuring Cecil's absence could be good for business. Then Murray's cell phone rang, a call from his own dealership, and he left the room to answer it. The teenager who took the cars to the wash had stolen another roll of quarters. Murray ordered his immediate dismissal and returned to the living room, where he found Irene sitting alone.

"Where'd Cecil go?" he asked her.

"Said he was going to set up camp."

"What a presumptuous shit," Murray said. "He won't use more than his third of the property."

"He doesn't seem too bad," Irene said. "Different than I imagined."

It was then that Murray saw Cecil in the backyard,

the horse standing next to him. He was emptying the saddlebags and pulling things from his oversized pack. Irene stood up from the floor and joined Murray by the window.

"He does seem different," Murray said. "Calmer maybe, but more fucked up."

They watched in silence as Cecil hammered stakes, anchoring a nylon teepee to the ground — the contraption looked like it might've been ordered from a catalogue specifically catering to midlife crises.

"What's he doing?" Murray asked.

"Setting up camp, I guess," Irene said.

✵

During dinner that evening, Cecil complimented Murray's game hen marinade. He drank only one glass of wine. He didn't mention the saltiness of Irene's salad dressing. This pleasant behavior did little to put Murray at ease — he'd always been unnerved by kindness from Cecil.

They had nearly finished eating when Cecil said, "I've been doing some research on our family."

Irene nodded and Murray forked a spare arugula leaf into his mouth. Although typically an aggressive eater, Murray ate with even more vigor in Cecil's presence — it was a superb means of avoiding conversation.

"We're Indians," Cecil said, in an exhausted way, as though he'd long been burdened by the information.

"What do you mean?" Irene asked.

"We're a quarter Quapaw. I found pictures of our long-lost grandfather online." He tugged at the beaded

166

headband he was wearing.

Murray picked at the skin of his game hen. He'd known about their Native American heritage for years — everyone in the family did. The grandfather Cecil referred to had accumulated considerable wealth selling life insurance in Jonesboro.

"That's wonderful, Cecil," Irene said. "I looked for information about my family at the library for seniors but couldn't find anything. Most of our funds go to discreetly smutty novels."

Murray swallowed his food. He knew Cecil was expecting him to respond. He finally asked, "Does this have anything to do with your sudden interest in the pond?"

"I've been honoring our ancestors for nearly a year now," Cecil said.

"Your reverence could hardly be more offensive," Murray said. "Quapaw didn't order their houses from Cabela's."

Cecil spoke to Irene, undeterred: "And then a couple of months ago it occurred to me that I wasn't honoring my most immediate ancestor. When all of this pond robber stuff started it seemed like more than a coincidence — I have the chance to protect Dad's legacy."

"That's really beautiful, Cecil," Irene said, her voice maintaining a polite flatness.

Murray excused himself from the table and went to the kitchen sink, where he washed his hands, the splash drowning out Cecil's voice, the heat scalding the pads of his fingers. To remain away from the table he started a pot of coffee. As it brewed he could hear Cecil and Irene laughing.

Cecil had, for as long as Murray could remember, resented the pond. He'd been the only family member to resist the pond outings, to tell their dad he didn't want canned meat as a present, didn't care about catfish. According to Cecil, their father had taken better care of the fish than his children. The truth was, Cecil had been the worst fisherman of the four Thornwiler kids, his restlessness causing him to reel in too frequently, his clumsiness knotting up lines. On the rare occasion when Cecil had landed a fish, he'd fiddled with it on the muddy bank, mangling their father's strict catch-and-release procedures.

And yet when Murray returned to the dinner table, Cecil was showing Irene a topographic map that charted the pond robberies. He'd marked the incidents with color-coordinated stickers — red for bream, blue for catfish, green for bass. Cecil claimed that the incidents were getting closer, that they were moving toward their farm.

"The map is ridiculous, Cecil," Murray said. "Who'd plan that carefully?"

Cecil responded as though he'd been waiting on the question: "A downtrodden fish farmer, desperate to cut down on the competition. A bitter divorcé, the former spouse of someone who loved to fish. A radicalized environmental type, someone hell-bent on eliminating non-native species."

Murray couldn't help but dismiss these theories —

how could something as silly as blowing up fish have any order, any predictability? But dealing with Cecil necessitated a careful balance of firmness and appeasement. Outright opposition had never worked very well — Cecil was too stubborn, too petty. It was best to placate him, to a certain degree, and then try to influence him.

"That's what they want you to think, Cecil," Murray said.

"What who wants me to think?"

"The fish terrorists — they want you to live in fear. And it's obvious they're succeeding."

For a long moment the three of them were silent. Their silverware scrapes and salivary noises spoke to spine-deep discomfort. After a loud guggle of wine, Irene said, "Cecil gave me a pill to help with my carpal tunnel. He said that it will — how'd you put it?"

"It expresses the muscles," Cecil said, and then the two of them laughed.

Murray asked what the pills were.

"They're painkillers," Cecil said, handing Murray the bottle.

Murray examined the label carefully, pretending to know something about medications.

"I have something to show you, Murray," Cecil said, standing up from the table.

Murray followed him outside. Cecil went into his teepee and returned with a longbow. Its cams were made of polished sycamore, a deep red color, its string waxy and smooth. Everything associated with Cecil seemed to take on the appearance of a prop, something to be looked at rather than used. The bow belonged on the wall of a resort lobby, Murray thought.

Cecil tugged an arrow from the quiver and locked it onto the string. Then he handed it to Murray and told him to give it a try.

"Afraid I don't have a target on hand," Murray said.

Cecil pointed to the remains of an oak tree that had been struck by lightning. "Try out that stump over there."

"Won't it ruin the arrow?" Murray asked.

"It'll definitely ruin the arrow. But there are more arrows to be ruined."

Murray drew the bow. His arms trembled against the weight of the string. When he tried to relax the cams, the string yanked forward with just enough momentum to softly launch the arrow, lobbing it toward the garden.

"Looks like that arrow's safe," Cecil said.

❋

The next morning Cecil moved his camp to the pond, and for a few days Murray and Irene resumed their usual lives. Murray anticipated contact from Cecil — a panicked phone call or a doorbell ring in the middle of the night — but heard nothing. By the end of the week Murray's curiosity outweighed his desire to avoid Cecil, so he drove out to the pond.

When he arrived, Murray saw Cecil's teepee in the shade of an oak tree. In nearby grass, rocks were circled into a fire pit, which was straddled by roasting sticks.

And on the edge of the woods was a roughshod outbuilding — a latrine, Murray guessed. For a long moment Murray sat in his truck, considering Cecil's work — one way or another, his brother had put together a respectable camp.

When Murray climbed out of his truck, a breeze tousled the grass at his knees, the wind prickly with the morning's wetness. Alice, saddled as always, grazed at the edge of camp. Murray found Cecil inside the teepee, rearranging pine needles to cushion the floor.

"Back's been acting up again," Cecil said.

"Is it a lumbar issue?" Murray asked.

"I guess it could be."

"It's usually a lumbar issue," Murray said.

"I was just about to take my bow and hunt for supper," Cecil said. "I found an old creek bed rabbits like. It's thick with them."

"What are they doing in there?" Murray asked.

"Jittering, mostly," Cecil said. "Scratching, every once in a while."

"You don't have to hunt for dinner," Murray said. "We still have some game hens leftover."

Cecil started to speak, stopped himself, and finally said, "I get a thrill from the hunt."

"Didn't you like the game hens?" Murray asked.

"Wild rabbits are healthier, anyway," Cecil said.

Murray nodded toward the pond. "You could eat catfish."

Cecil laughed at that blasphemous notion, at the thought of breaking their father's rule, but then, slowly, his expression changed.

"I wonder what they taste like," he said.

"I've got an old pole or two at the house," Murray said.

Cecil left his teepee, went over to Alice, and pulled his bow from the saddlebag. When he returned, he handed Murray a Styrofoam carton. "This is the last of the chicken liver. Good and rotten. If you handle it, I'll take care of the rest."

They walked to the pond's edge. Cecil nocked an arrow and nodded his readiness. Murray lobbed a piece of chicken liver a few feet from the bank and Cecil drew the bowstring. The two of them waited, staring at the meat, but the water was still. Just after Cecil gave up, a fish snapped the liver from the surface, a splash rising, its wake cresting into the bank.

"Shit," they said, at the same time, with the same inflection.

"We have any liver left?" Cecil asked. They were two brothers with an idea they couldn't relinquish — Murray was reminded, vaguely, of the time they'd gone out to the highway to shoot slingshots at passing cars.

Murray peeled open the lid, looked inside. "Only a couple of small pieces."

"Toss them both out," Cecil said.

"Seems risky," Murray said, but he pulled the rotten scraps from the carton and Cecil readied the bow. Murray cupped both pieces in his hand and pitched them into the water. As soon as they landed a fish bobbed up and Cecil fired. The shaft of the arrow slapped the water as the tip punched into the fish's head. Its body rolled, sending the arrow upright, briefly, before it wilted to the water's surface.

"I didn't think you'd actually hit one," Murray said.

Murray stood by while his brother removed his moccasins and retrieved the fish. Afterwards Cecil built a fire and prepared to cook, and Murray lured Alice to the fire pit with Gobstoppers. He climbed onto her back and watched as Cecil used the arrow as a skewer, holding the fish over the flame.

They were silent as the fish cooked, the quiet holding the surprise, the spontaneity, of their harvest. It was rare for them to be quiet in each other's company — they'd always used words as a wedge, a means of maintaining distance.

"You're going to burn our catch," Murray said.

Cecil pushed the fish deeper into the flame, its grease ticking into the fire, turning out a dark, sweet-smelling smoke.

"You think it'll be any good?" Cecil asked.

"Hard to say," Murray said. "But I bet we'll be the first folks in Izard County to have a dinner of Japanese catfish."

Cecil pulled the fish from the flame and examined it. He tugged on the pectoral fin and it peeled away, the size and shape of a potato chip. He put the piece in his mouth and chewed slowly, his chin bobbing.

"You've got to try this," Cecil said.

Murray climbed off Alice. When Cecil extended the fish, Murray tore away a slender strip of skin. Then

Cecil raised the fish to his mouth and chomped into its side, skin and all.

"It's all right," Cecil said, his cheeks slick with grease. "Considering we don't have any seasoning or anything."

Murray nibbled on the meat attached to the underside of the skin. He wanted the meat to be revelatory, to tell him something, but all it revealed was oily bitterness. Still, when Cecil offered the fish, Murray took another strip. He peeled the meat with his teeth and dropped the leftover skin into the fire, which had steadied to a low orange flame. They settled into another silence while they ate the fish, bland as it was, to the bones.

✳

Murray spent the next few evenings at the pond with Cecil — and did so willingly. Their estrangement had taken place slowly; small disappointments and frustrations hardened, year after year, into resentment — but now, sharing dusks beside the pond, they chiseled at those fossilized feelings.

After Murray detailed his failings as a father, Cecil said, "Dentists aren't *that* bad, Murray. Sure, they always seem a little like perverts, the way they fish around in people's mouths, but you could've raised insurance men."

On another evening, Cecil told Murray he'd taken leave from work to manage his prescription drug addiction.

"Let me see the pills," Murray said.

Cecil handed him the bottle.

Murray threw the bottle into the pond. It plopped into the water and then bobbed on the surface. Cecil stared at it for a moment before saying, "That was a moving gesture, but I have a bunch of refills."

"That'll stop you for a while. Maybe give you a fresh start."

Cecil pointed to the bottle. "I think it's coming back."

The bottle, its lid still intact, floated toward them. They watched it drift, the wind guiding it back to shore. Cecil went to the water's edge and grabbed the bottle, shook the moisture from it, and stuffed it back in his pocket.

Things progressed in this affable manner for nearly a week. Indeed, the two of them fared wonderfully until one day, after a lunch of pimento cheese sandwiches, Murray found Cecil standing in the doorway of his former bedroom. He was studying the mounted family fish. A few months earlier, Murray had polished Cecil's fish, thinking he could improve its color. Now the skin was sickly and brittle — pieces had flaked onto Murray's desk.

"What an awful fucking fish," Cecil said. "I'd forgotten how bad it was."

Murray started to say it wasn't that bad but looked up at the thing and thought better of it. "I think it's gotten worse," he said. "The taxidermist fucked up."

"No, it was always awful. By the time I was twelve I'd stopped looking at it because it was so ugly."

"Look how short the dorsal fins on Sarah's are,"

Murray said. "That can't be normal."

Cecil didn't respond.

After a lengthy silence, Cecil asked, "Where's your fish?"

Murray deliberated before he spoke. "Do you have any more pills?" he asked.

Cecil pulled the bottle from his pocket, held it out to Murray.

Murray shook a pill out and handed it to Cecil.

"What's this for?"

"You're going to need it," Murray said.

❈

Alice grazed in the high Bermuda near the family cemetery while Murray and Cecil walked through the rows of stones. Most of their relatives were memorialized with squat limestone markers, the engravings diminished by time. But in the middle of the cemetery was a sizable marble slab, a monument fit for a courthouse lawn. It was their father's gravestone.

Above the frank lettering of the name — HORACE THORNWILER — hung Murray's fish, the colossal first catch. Murray and Cecil stared up at it.

"I don't understand why your fish is hanging on Dad's headstone," Cecil said.

"It's what Dad wanted," Murray said.

"It wasn't on there when we buried him."

"The taxidermist had to weatherize it first," Murray said.

Alice trampled through the open gate of the cemetery. She plucked grass from the grave of their great aunt Lucille, a woman Murray remembered for her tendency to wear bread sacks over her shoes when it was raining.

Murray tried not to notice, but Cecil's eyes were wet, puffy.

"Why didn't you tell me?" Cecil asked.

Murray touched the mount, testing its sealant.

"It's just a fish," he said.

✳

Cecil was quiet on the ride back to the house. Murray found Irene in the living room and took a seat beside her. A minute later, Cecil passed them and continued down the hallway toward the bedrooms. Murray leaned forward, watching as Cecil entered the office. He came out carrying his mounted fish and passed through the front door without a word.

Murray turned the television on — the real estate channel, blueprints of a log cabin. Irene went to the foyer and watched Cecil out the window.

"What's he doing?" Murray asked.

"Cramming his fish into the saddlebag," Irene said. "I feel bad for him."

"That's what he wants — someone to feel bad for him."

"Is he leaving?" she asked.

"He didn't say. But if he wants to leave, we should let him."

"Now he's brushing his hair with the mane brush he just used on Alice," Irene said. "You should do something."

177

Murray went to the foyer, stood beside her. They watched as Cecil rode away. The mounted tail protruded from the saddlebag, swinging in rhythm with the horse's steps, as though his fish were swimming downward.

✻

An hour after Cecil left, the phone rang.

"Have you checked your pond lately?" the caller asked. It was Larry Gilmore, who lived a mile away from Murray and was known for his whispery telephone voice. Murray pinched his ear against the receiver and said, "My brother checked it this morning."

"Well, I just went out to mine. Nearly flopped over myself and joined the fish."

"What're you going to do?" Murray asked.

"Get nets and clean up best I can. If I just leave them out there they'll stink like a fat lady's fingers after the seafood buffet."

After hanging up, Murray left his house to look for Cecil. It was about five miles to the Jacksons' horse farm, but he didn't know how long that would take on horseback — somewhere between thirty minutes and four hours, he guessed. He drove the winding single-lane highway that led into town, scanning the road's wide shoulders. He didn't see any sign of Cecil until he turned off the highway and traveled along a dirt road toward the Jacksons' barn. There he found Cecil walking beside Alice, his steps stiff, legs bowed. Murray pulled up beside him, rolled down his window.

"What're you doing?" Murray asked.

"Bad case of saddle soreness."

Murray nodded.

"Feels like a pack of coyotes gnawing on my groin," Cecil said.

"Larry Gilmore called — pond robber got his pond. Thought you might want to help me protect ours."

"Why didn't you just call me?" Cecil pointed to a bluetooth earpiece.

Murray pumped his brakes, stopping and going in order to stay even with Cecil. "Would you have answered?"

"Probably not."

"Who cares that my fish was bigger? And healthier? And prettier?"

"You do," Cecil said, tugging at the crotch of his blue jeans.

"Well, it means less to me than it used to."

"You enjoyed taking me out there," Cecil said.

"It wasn't in his will," Murray said.

Cecil stopped but Alice kept walking, her reins yanking him forward.

"It was my idea to put the fish on there. I thought his tombstone was a little dull without it."

"I'm starting to think that owning a horse is a lot of trouble," Cecil said.

"Let's stop this guy," Murray said.

"I did leave my teepee out there," Cecil said. "And Cabela's has sold out of them." He plodded along for another ten paces, every step scattering gravel, until he asked, "Will you ride Alice back?"

When they made it to the levee, Murray set out to
gather firewood. As he headed toward the brush, the
sun dripped behind the treed horizon. For a moment
the world seemed brighter than before, the sky opened
by the sun's departure. Murray gathered a bundle of
hickory limbs and returned to the levee, where he found
Cecil squinting at his pond robber map.

"What kind of fish did Larry Gilmore have?" Cecil
asked.

"Largemouth, mostly," Murray said. "A few blue-
gills, too."

Cecil contemplated this before pulling out both
green and blue stickers. "That's the third bass pond this
week," he said.

Murray dropped the wood onto the levee and sat
down. "I'm sorry about the headstone," he said.

Cecil nodded, distracted.

"I did it about six months after he died. Not too long
after I moved out here."

"You're overselling it, Murray," Cecil said. "I know it
was in his will."

"Then why'd you come back to the pond?"

"Because it was nice of you to lie about it. And
because I like camping."

Murray considered the answer. Then he said, "Irene
offered to bring us some magazines from the senior
citizen library. Something to do while we wait."

"It'll be dark within the hour," Cecil said, looking up

from the map. "And we won't be waiting much longer anyhow."

As though summoned by Cecil's words, the noise of a vehicle clattered through the twilight, an engine punching into the evening breeze — it was an ATV, Murray could tell. The machine emerged on the far end of the levee, headed toward them.

"Shit," said Murray.

"Who is it?"

"Somebody on a three-wheeler."

Cecil's throat quacked — a moan interrupted by a gulp. "Three-wheelers are very dangerous," he said.

As the vehicle continued toward them, Murray tried to imagine a person reckless enough to imperil himself on three wheels. Alice stopped eating grass and joined them on the tire-trodden ground of the levee; she too was unnerved by the approaching noise. Fifty yards away the three-wheeler stopped and the driver cut the engine.

The quiet of twilight now seemed amplified, new. For a moment the trespasser sat on his ATV, looking over the peaceful surface of the pond. Then he climbed off and drifted toward them, still examining the pond. He was balding and had the angular body of a teenager; this contradiction led Murray to guess, correctly, that the fellow was in his late twenties. He was dressed in the gear of an overeager fisherman — a pair of hip boots, a tackle vest — and he carried an ordinary fishing pole.

It occurred to Murray that he'd hardly considered

the physical presence of the pond robber, whose behavior had been so stealthy and efficient as to seem made not of actions but words — printed in the newspaper, whispered over the telephone, clicked on the internet. No, the pond robber had not been a bodily figure in Murray's imagination — he'd been an idea with dynamite.

Now, as this man neared them, he asked, "Mind if I cast a line?"

Cecil nodded in an inscrutable way.

Murray said, "We typically don't allow it."

"I'll catch and release," the man said, smiling. "Always do." He had a small birthmark in the cropped hair over his ear. A white patch, like paint spatter.

"We don't fish this pond," Murray said. "Not any good, anyhow." He'd tried to sound relaxed, but instead he'd come close to replicating his frigid performance of a single line in his high school's production of *West Side Story*.

The man nodded. Then he turned to look over the pasture, like maybe he'd find another pond. Murray followed his gaze. The sage grass flickering in a barely detectable breeze.

"Have you tried fishing it with one of these?" the man asked. In his palm was a soft plastic lure, the size and shape of a plug of tobacco.

"What's that?" Cecil asked.

"It's called a Getz-It," the man said.

"How do you spell that?" Cecil asked.

The man spelled — with careful enunciation —

while Murray continued his silent assessment. Was this the man who'd flustered the whole county? The fellow who was, at that very moment, wavering as to whether the lure's proper spelling called for a 'Z' or an 'S'?

"Either way," the man said, "they carry them at the bait shop over by Super Wok King Buffet."

"Don't they have the driest eggrolls?" Cecil asked.

"When that bait doesn't work, I use this one," the man said, and began fumbling with a vest pocket. "This damned Velcro — always screws up my timing."

While the man groped the pocket, Cecil said, "I hate the stuff. Had to get a new wallet."

The Velcro ripped open, finally, and the man pulled out a stick of dynamite. It was stout as a church candle, a twine-like fuse dangling from its tip. "It's made for underwater mining," the pond robber said. "Fuse burns when it's submerged same as it would in the Mohave."

"They don't sell that one at the bait store," Cecil said.

Murray winced.

"It's up to you two," the pond robber said. "Which one of these baits would you like me to tie on?"

"The Getz-It might do the trick," Cecil said.

Murray nodded his agreement, and the pond robber tied on the plastic bait. He cast to the center of the pond and jigged the bait, reeling slowly. Murray hoped he'd catch something — that might buy them some time. But what would they do with time? Maybe Cecil could take up the longbow, but Murray wasn't thrilled with the idea of threatening a dynamite-wielding man with a prehistoric weapon.

And so he simply stood beside Cecil, watching the pond robber. The man fished calmly, eyes focused on the water. Murray noticed the line tensing, lifting from the surface, but the pond robber remained still, his rod tip lowered. Just when Murray was about to mention the tightening line, the pond robber yanked the pole upward, its fiberglass arcing. He reeled slowly, his hands working against the weight of his catch.

Murray and Cecil moved closer. The pond robber pulled the fish toward the bank, his line zigzagging over the surface. With the fish halfway in, he turned toward them. "Who wants to finish this thing?"

"It's all yours," Murray said, adopting Cecil's friendly — and apparently successful — tone.

He extended the rod. "One of you really ought to take this — she's a big mother."

"You hooked it," Cecil said.

"But it's your pond," the pond robber said.

Cecil stepped forward and took the pole. His hands fumbled as he started reeling. Murray thought of all those times during their childhood when Cecil had failed to land his fish, their dad screaming over his shoulder. As the fish neared the bank Cecil's reeling slowed, his arms flagging.

"Keep your rod tip up," the pond robber said. "Let her make a run or two and she'll wear out."

Cecil's breathing was heavy, his face red, but he continued to crank. Then, all at once, the fish rose to the surface, where it lay on its side, exhausted from the fight. Cecil pulled it the last few feet and the pond robber hoisted the fish from the mud. It was the biggest the pond had ever produced — ten pounds, easily. With the pond robber holding its head belly-high, its tail slapped the mud.

"Damn, what a fish," the pond robber said. "Just what kind of catfish is this?"

"A Japanese breed," Murray said.

Cecil feigned modesty, but Murray could see the pride in his brother's posture, like his whole body was swallowing a smile.

"What do y'all want to do with it?" the pond robber asked. He wrestled with the hook, which was planted deep in the fish's mouth. The fish croaked, its empty gills flexing.

"I'd like to get it mounted," Cecil said.

"It's a big one, all right," Murray said. "But I think we should throw it back."

Cecil faced Murray, smiling in an angry way. "We shot a fish and ate it right here on this bank."

Behind Cecil the pond robber continued to dig inside the fish's mouth. "You better make up your minds," he said. "Assuming I can even get this hook out."

"Are you worried I'm going to put it on his gravestone?" Cecil asked.

Here was Murray's chance to let Cecil have a trophy of his own, to right his brother's relationship with their father, to relieve him of decades of shame. The pond robber freed the hook from the gullet and raised the fish. Held upright in the waning light, the fish looked, to Murray at least, like one of the patients at his mother's nursing home; its eyes were crazed, bulging with the knowledge of a long life.

"Make up your goddamn mind, Murray," Cecil said.

"Aren't we trying to honor him?" Murray asked.

Cecil didn't answer. His expression was disorienting — a boy's disappointment on an old man's face.

The fish wriggled in the pond robber's grip. He transferred the fish from one hand to the other, moving closer to the pond, his toes nicking the water.

"It wouldn't be right to break tradition," Murray said.

Cecil made a noise like a sigh. Then he looked back at the pond robber and gestured toward the pond, his arm sluggish.

The pond robber heaved the fish into the water. Once it had submerged, he backed away and trotted down the levee toward his three-wheeler. Murray and Cecil stood there baffled by his departure, until they turned to the pond and saw the glow of a lit fuse, light bubbling inside the fish's mouth.

Even the Trees Were Sweating

We were on the interstate headed from Memphis to Little
Rock when the cars in front of us mashed their brakes. I
mashed mine too and the empty serving bowl in the
backseat clonked against the console. I checked the
rearview mirror, hoping the cars back there wouldn't
pile into us.

"Shit," Janie said. She was distracted, reading something on her phone. She was always reading something
on her phone, mostly medical websites and health
blogs, like she thought the articles might suffuse her
body with the nutrients it needed, the nourishment it
lacked.

"Was that my mom's serving bowl?" Janie asked.

"I think so," I said. "But I'm a little preoccupied."

"I should've put it up here with me. We can't let it
break."

The traffic accumulated quickly, a long wall of semis
and minivans, coupes and motorcycles. It was the
Friday before the Fourth, the road packed with people
traveling somewhere to cook out and drink beer and
shoot fireworks, to participate in rituals so clichéd that
they'd taken on a certain novelty. Janie and I were
headed to Little Rock to spend the holiday with her
parents — they seized every opportunity to be around
Janie, to feed her, to protect her. They believed they
could, through the sheer force of their concern, coerce

Janie into health and happiness.

At first the drivers were impatient, everyone crawling along, brake lights flashing, cars getting closer and closer. Drivers leaned forward, hands gripping steering wheels like reins. Passengers stretched their arms over their heads in a demonstrative, yawn-inducing way. The truck driver next to us held a radio to his mouth, his lips shaping curse words.

After the traffic had completely stopped, we sat there in silence for a few minutes. The highway, our rapid movement from one place to another, had given us permission to be quiet, but once we were sitting still, the silence was tenuous. I realized that my foot was still mashed against the brake pedal. I shifted into park and my car rocked forward, back. I scooted my seat back, raised my hands toward the air conditioning vents. They were blowing warm air. It was disgustingly hot — July in Arkansas.

"What's going on?" Janie asked.

"We need Freon, I think."

"No, with the traffic. Why're we stopped?"

"I don't know," I said.

"My parents are waiting on us," she said.

I wanted to say something cruel. I wanted to ask if her parents might starve while waiting for us. But this is what I said: "Maybe you should give them a call."

There was a proximity, an intimacy, in the traffic, our cars closing in on one another until there was nowhere left to go. We'd squeezed out every spare inch of empty highway, it seemed, and now we were stuck.

"This heat is making me sick," she said

The therapists we'd seen together had told me not to change my behavior, to keep our conversations as natural as possible — a suggestion that made me acutely aware of everything that came out of my mouth.

"Maybe we'll get going soon," I said.

A minute later the driver of the eighteen-wheeler beside us opened his door and climbed down from the high cab.

"Where's he going?" Janie asked as he passed by her window.

I watched him in the rearview. He walked in the narrow space between cars, turning sideways between sideview mirrors. He walked fifty yards until he came to another eighteen-wheeler. Then he raised himself to the passenger door and climbed inside.

"That's not a good sign," I said.

"A good sign for what?"

"The truckers must know something."

"Based on what?"

"Truckers always know something."

Janie leaned her seat back, put her forearm over her brow.

I noticed a man on a motorcycle driving very slowly toward us, the wrong direction, on the highway shoulder. He wasn't wearing a helmet, and as he approached I saw that he was old, probably mid-seventies, his white suspenders stretched over a navy blue tee-shirt.

I rolled down the window and asked what was going on.

"I can't hear you," he said. "Engine's too loud."

"What's going on?" I yelled.

"I'm getting out of here," he said. "They should have their own highway system."

I nodded, though I had no clue what he was talking about.

He took my nodding, apparently, as a sign to turn his motorcycle off. When the engine stopped thumping, the old man's voice was somber. "There are so many eighteen-wheelers on this stretch of highway. Their tires leave grooves in the road. Was only a matter of time before a couple got tangled up."

"There's been a wreck?"

He nodded. "I live just past the next exit," he said, tilting his head the direction we were facing. I looked forward, noticed a low wall of smoke along the horizon, an eraser smear against the afternoon blue. "I never come out on this highway," he said, patting his motor-cycle. "I'm just a minnow. Don't like to go swimming with the sharks."

The old man and I stared at each other a moment. He hooked his thumb under his suspender strap and lifted it and let it snap back onto his shoulder. He started his motorcycle and yelled, "I knew better than to come out here."

I watched him leave in the sideview mirror, until he stopped again a few cars behind us.

"Is that smoke?" Janie asked.

The smoke was a bit higher and a bit grayer than before, thinning as it rose toward the sun. It was three o'clock and we were headed west. I leaned forward and looked up; the sun seemed wet, nebulous, like a cell under a microscope. Janie and I were cooking beneath our windshield, even with the air conditioner roaring.

Janie reached to the back of her head, pulling a rubber band from her wrist and twisting it around a wad of hair. A limp ponytail fell onto her shoulder, the hair at her temples flattened by sweat.

"How much longer can it take?" she asked. "I'm burning up."

"Maybe you should call your parents," I said. "I don't want them waiting on us to eat."

"I feel too sick to call them," she said. She never felt like calling them, never felt like calling anyone.

I was pulling my phone from my pocket when the driver-side door of the car directly in front of us swung open and a bearded man in suit and tie climbed out. He had a nervous cleaned-up look, like a man headed to his divorce hearing. He approached slowly, hands in pockets, and as he neared my window he adopted an upright manly posture, as though maybe he was about to ask the score of the big game.

"What's going on?" the man asked.

"There's been a wreck," I said. "That's what the man on the motorcycle said."

"I saw the smoke," he said. "Must be pretty bad to come to a full-on stop like this."

"A couple of semis, apparently."

"I hope we're not out here much longer," he said. "This heat is awful."

Janie mumbled something I couldn't understand and then she leaned over the console, reaching into the backseat.

"How far's the nearest gas station?" I asked the man.

He pointed to Janie. "Is she all right?"

She was holding her head over her mother's serving bowl, neck muscles flexing as she gagged.

I turned back to the man and said, "She'll be fine."

I expected him to leave but he just stood there watching Janie. I didn't know what to say to him. "Could you give us a minute?" I asked.

"Of course," he said. He pulled a handkerchief from the inside pocket of his suit jacket. "This is brand new. Y'all can have it."

As he walked away, Janie vomited into the serving bowl, her body convulsing. It unnerved me how quiet she was, how I wouldn't have known she was vomiting had I not been watching. It unnerved me how delicate, how pretty, she was even then, as her afternoon snack of honey-drenched marshmallows spilled into her mother's serving bowl. I didn't know whether to place my hand on her sweaty neck, whether to grip her curved shoulders. I didn't know how to comfort her and didn't know if I wanted to.

I waited for her to finish and then handed her the man's handkerchief. She held it for a moment, lifting it carefully up to her nose.

"It smells like cigarettes," she said, as she wiped her cheeks.

For a moment we sat there quietly, both of us

staring forward. Janie adjusted the sun visor but it didn't really do any good. The sun was omnipresent.

News of the wreck had spread, it seemed, and a few restless people climbed out of their vehicles. A skinny woman got out of the car behind us and performed a series of runner's stretches. In the median a father and son tossed a Frisbee, their feet slinging roadside gravel. Several cars ahead, a couple of boys in fraternity tee-shirts opened the tailgate of a truck and sat down on it, gesturing cigarettes up to their mouths as they talked.

"These people are creeping me out," Janie said.

She was right. It was an odd scene, people milling around on the interstate, out in the middle of nowhere.

She pointed to the thicket beside the road. "Is that man peeing?"

"Janie, are you okay?"

She looked out her window in an affected way, like she was studying the mudflaps of the eighteen-wheeler beside us.

When she didn't answer, I climbed out of the car. I stood there with the door open, the sun firm against my skin, humidity clinging to the cotton of my shirt. It was so hot that everything around us seemed to be perspiring — even the trees were sweating.

Janie leaned over the console and asked, "What're you doing, Nate? We could get going anytime."

"Just stretching out a little," I said. "At least there's a breeze out here."

"Please get back in the car," she said.

She looked like she was about to cry, to scream and

beg and throw a fit. And I didn't know it then, but that's what I wanted — to hurt someone so skilled at hurting herself.

I closed the door and started down the highway shoulder, headed in the direction of the smoke. I walked past luxury sedans and horse trailers, fishing boats and SUVs. The majority of people remained in their cars, drivers still gripping steering wheels, passengers still staring at phones. But some had turned their cars off, had decided to wait it out in the heat.

I heard a sizzling flare and then a snap above me. I recognized the noise immediately. A bottle rocket. I saw another one shoot up, pop, directly over the highway. I traced its trajectory backward to the launching point and then headed that direction, crossing the highway behind the shoe-polished windows of a Suburban, then a beat-up Toyota.

I'd expected to encounter kids, teenagers maybe, who'd decided to pass time shooting fireworks, but instead I found a middle-aged woman dressed in a long-sleeve denim shirt, her hair the dingy tint of aquarium water. She stood there alone, a pile of bottle rockets lying at her feet.

After I greeted her, she handed me a single bottle rocket and a cigarette lighter. The stick was flimsy under the weight of its gunpowder packet, limp as a roadside daisy. I lit the bottle rocket and cocked my arm, prepared to toss it. I waited, as the flame curled up the wick, as sparks flecked onto my wrist, for just the right time to let go.

A Thousand Distant Radios

On the day my granddad died I went down to the basement to be with his body. It was quaint down there, dusty cinder blocks and high windows, like a bedroom on a concrete yacht. There were empty wine bottles and books with broken spines and cast-off paintings, everything chalked in long-ago smoke, the layers of so many lung-collapsing drags. In the floor lay the body of the smoker — he was the drinker and reader and painter too — who'd tumbled over that morning and left me to tidy it all up.

✣

There were cartons of cigarettes stacked waist-high around the room, leaning towers of factory tobacco, a supply big enough to back up three hospitals with bodies. They'd been delivered on a forklift driven by R.J. Reynolds himself, one night after he and my granddad shot pistols at the moon.

I picked up a carton and took a long contemplative look, the way I reckoned you were supposed to look at dead people's stuff. I peeled away the silky plastic wrapping and lifted the carton to my nose, the smell faint as wintertime nostalgia. Then I pulled out a pack and tucked it into the chest pocket of my tee-shirt.

My granddad said the first drag was the sweetest, so he'd smoke them one long drag a piece and stub them out. He'd toss the dead cigarettes in the hollowed out noggin of his stuffed buffalo. It had been gutshot by a drunken Annie Oakley. The beast had dragged a bullet-punched rope of intestines halfway across the plains, blood matting its wooly hide while it weaved through miles of wheat. It finally buckled over at the foot of the Rocky Mountains. Annie's last kill. When I'd ask my granddad more about Annie and about how he ended up with her last buffalo he'd tell me that if this country were the body of a man, the Rocky Mountains would be his liver, gnarled up and hardened by the rest of the nation's troubles.

✸

I stripped my granddad down before I did anything else. I took off his old army waistcoat and I took off his plaid shirt and I took off his Dockers.

I took off his hat. It was a burgundy trilby, a relic of relics, its fabric skull-worn, passed down from his father the Baptist pastor. It was the only thing he'd inherited from his father, my granddad said.

I took off his moccasins. He'd won them in a poker game with the son of Red Cloud, that old warrior who'd fought for Montana and fought for Wyoming before he fought for his reservation, unsatisfied with the slivers of land his people had been rationed by the U.S. govern-ment, that old warrior for democracy. I tugged at the socks to get them off his feet, their stiff wool clinging to bony shins.

✸

I had my dead granddad naked save for his Hanes, his body stark white against the crimson rug he brought back from World War II. It was a prize rug, a Persian rug, the spoils of a boxing match with General Patton.

I lifted his body onto a table and rolled it to the center of the room — it was an old operating table he'd used during his time as a Hollywood acupuncturist. He used to tell me he'd pricked blood out of more starlets than Bogart himself. I'd ask, but what about Rhett Butler? Did you prick more than him too, Granddad? And he'd just smile, his teeth sharp like sanded pearls.

❈

Next to his body his clothes seemed excessive, looked like more than he could have ever worn, like just standing up in them could've knocked him to the floor. Lying on that table, his skin embered in the light of a naked bulb, he could've been any dead thing. He could've been a trout, still stream-cold and striated, waiting for a fillet blade. He could've been a storebought Christmas turkey, clenched up skin and legs splayed out, ready for the oven's heat. But he wasn't those things and he wasn't any other thing except for my dead granddad.

❈

I found the big rusty can in the corner and hauled it over to him. When I tipped the can a splash of gasoline gurgled out. It slicked the grizzled white of his chest hair. I rubbed the gas into his skin with my hands, varnished his flesh with a glassy purple, my hands streaking through the clumped hair. I poured a second splash of gasoline and kept rubbing. I massaged his naked body until he glistened like a Florida poolwife, the fuel's bitter chemicals chapping my hands. I rubbed until the gas made me woozy, its tang wafting up, numbing my nostrils, falling into my lungs. I rubbed until I couldn't tell who the rubbing was for, my dead granddad or me.

※

Even drenched in gasoline, my dead granddad looked thirsty, so I grabbed him by his hair and lifted his head forward. I pulled his mouth open with the hook of my finger, my knuckle on hard tongue, and I snaked the spout of the gas can into his mouth. His teeth chomped around the nozzle as I tipped the gas can toward him, poured slowly, listening to the gasoline gargle in the back of his throat.

It funneled into him. I didn't know where it was going, didn't care whether it was headed for his lungs or his stomach. I just poured until he was full, until his body swelled with fluid, until the gas pooled inside his mouth and spilled onto his chest, its froth bubbling down his abdomen.

I set the gas can down and gripped him by the shoulders, shook him back and forth until I could hear the gasoline sloshing. Then I bent over his body, pressed my ear to his bloated belly, and listened to the gasoline slurp and fizz inside him. It sounded like the static of a thousand distant radios, like stories and sounds refusing to take shape.

※

I demolished the rest of the basement. I knocked over his bookcase. Glass shattered and spines broke and loose pages floated through the air like October leaves.

I kicked over the stacked cartons of cigarettes and they fell around the room like discarded dominoes. I tore through his paintings, mixed masterpieces with duds, made a mosaic of his whole painting career. I ripped down shelves of liquor, shelves of wine, sent bottles crashing to the floor. Dime store merlots fell with untouched single malts, their shards spraying across the room in an alcoholic mist.

When I was twelve years old, my dead granddad, still living then, had lowered me into the cellar with a stack of two-by-fours, a hammer, and a bag of nails. He'd told me that if I wanted to get out I'd build a set of stairs.

I went upstairs and searched through the house, catalogued everything he ever owned. Then I took it, all of it, down there to be with his body. I carried down the photographs that perched on his dresser, a picture of him and my dead grandmother standing on the deck of a Mississippi riverboat. I carried down easels and palettes and squeezed-out tubes of oil paints, carried down the paintings the Guggenheim had shipped back to him after a show. I carried down the pots my great uncle, his brother, had made for him, our family name engraved in the clay of their bases. I carried down his bed, his mattress, his recliner. I broke down his car, a '53 Studebaker, part by part, and I carried it down too. I had everything, his whole life, buried in that cellar, that coffin of a room.

✳

I bathed it all in gasoline. I walked around the room
with the gas can tilted, tiptoed through unwound strips
of film, squeezed by a transmission, sidestepped
through a maze of sunlight-scalded girly magazines,
doused it all in holy industrial blood — unleaded. I
filled up that bowl of a buffalo noggin and I drenched
his mattress and I soaked his piled-up clothes. I stopped
pouring when the can ran dry, the drops getting
smaller till they turned to specks, till they turned to
fumes.

✳

Halfway up the stairs I stopped, grabbed the pack of
cigarettes from my tee-shirt pocket. I opened it up,
pulled out an unfiltered Camel, and pressed it to my
lips. I lit the cigarette and took a long drag, its fragile
old smoke sinking into my lungs. I exhaled. My breaths
wisped up, out, until they disappeared. Then I flicked
the cigarette down. I watched fire skitter across the
concrete, curling up and around my dead granddad's
stuff. I listened to flames tick and spit, heave and pop, as
they grew.

✳

On the day my granddad died, he had so much history
it killed him, and I knew that if I wasn't careful, it
might swallow me up too. I climbed out of his basement
with nineteen cigarettes left to burn.

The author would like to thank Ian Golding again. The author would, lastly, like to thank the author Bess Winter, with whom he shares his home, his imagination, his future — and whose faith in his work is surpassed only by her faith in his ability to captain U-Haul trucks.

modified flattop: Ian Golding, Luke Geddes, Soon Wiley, Andrew Bales, Jamie Wilson, Matt Grolemund, Kallie Falandays, Joey Lemon, and Garrett Quinn. The author would like to thank two men who frequent Highland Coffee House in Cincinnati, Ohio: Dario Sulzman, a generous and insightful reader, and Jay the Barista, maker of delicious iced Thai coffees who, in four years, never once asked what the author was working on. The author would like to thank his lifelong friends and earliest readers in and from Arkansas, some of whom permitted him to live and work in their attics: Myles McDougal, Clark Baker, Will Alexander, and Madison Thompson. The author would like to thank the members of his nuclear family, who unfailingly supported and — with their understated peculiarity, senses of humor, and exuberance for 1990s life — inspired him. The author would like to thank his mother for escaping that long-distance telephone service pyramid scheme, and he would like to thank his father for offering convincing reassurances when his clients left threatening voicemails on the household answering machine. The author would like to thank his sister Jesse for laughing forcefully at his first attempt at absurdity — the Cookie Esposito persona the author adopted in the third grade. The author would additionally like to thank his elder sister, Julie, for a steady supply of pirated CDs and annual subscriptions to *Oxford American* when the author was in high school. The author would like to thank his publisher and editor, Mark Cunningham, whose creative vision, editorial acumen, and indefatigable commitment to a vibrant literary culture have brought this book into existence.

Acknowledgements

These stories originally appeared in the following publications:

Booth: "Preferred Signals, 1985"
Mid-American Review: "Things in Slow Motion"
The Carolina Quarterly: "The Knife Salesman"
Hobart: "Summering"
Catamaran: "Atlantic Blue"
Euphony: "Weight"
River Styx: "The Pond Robber"
Another Chicago Magazine: "Even the Trees Were Sweating"
Necessary Fiction: "A Thousand Distant Radios"

The author would like to thank the following people for their public support of this collection: Kevin Wilson, J. Robert Lennon, Elizabeth McKenzie, Kyle Minor, Scott Sparling, Margaret Malone, and Brian Trapp. The author would like to thank these editors and early champions of his work: Steve Himmer, Phil Sandick, Lindsay Starck, Robert Stapleton, J.T. Price, Aaron Burch, and Alan Heathcock. The author would like to thank Atelier26's publicist, Diane Prokop. The author would like to thank his many tolerant and faithful teachers: in Wichita — Margaret Dawe, Richard Spilman, Darren DeFrain, Katherine Vaz, and the late Steve Hathaway; in Cincinnati — Michael Griffith, Leah Stewart, and Chris Bachelder. The author would like to thank his Wichita classmates and friends, who took these stories seriously even though the author arrived in Kansas wearing cowboy boots and sporting a